All of Us with Our Pointless Worries and Inconsequential Dramas

Short Stories

Garry Crystal

Also by Garry Crystal
Fiction: Leaving London (Novel)

London – Saturday Night, Sunday Morning first published in Roadside Fiction (2014)

Garry Crystal is a freelance writer living in Scotland. His short stories and articles have appeared in print and online including Expats Post, The Andirondack Review, Turnrow Journal, Roadside Fiction and Orato. His first novel Leaving London is available now.

All content – GarryCrystal@2014

Contents

The Paris Quartet (Supporting Characters)

Waiting in the 11th Arrondissement
Anywhere But Here
All of Us with Our Pointless Worries and Inconsequential Dramas
Detours

Relationships

Strangers
Running with the Bulls
The Conversationalists
Kryptonite
The Route
Recorded Delivery
Grand Canyon

The Urban Jungle

How to be Depressed in London
The End of the Nineties
Filter Image
The Last Busker in London
London - Saturday Night, Sunday Morning
New York for Beginners

And When the Arguing's Over…

Hecklers
Algeciras
Appraising
Happily…Ever…
The Elephant Frowned
The Seawall

The Paris Quartet
(Supporting Characters)

Waiting in the 11th Arrondissement

The man seems nervous to me whereas the woman is much more relaxed. She walks confidently through the door, open, smiling, happy to be here. He, on the other hand is constantly looking elsewhere and checking out who is in the restaurant, which at this early hour is still quite empty. Parisians don't usually eat until much later in the evening and the woman had come in only hours earlier to book a table, taking what was on offer; eight o' clock on a Saturday night.

Damn. I cannot remember her name although I recognize the face, not a great start. Heading behind the desk I check the reservations book until her name appears. I know her from the neighbourhood. Actually I don't know her but I recognize her face. I've often seen her riding her bicycle, the one with the basket on the front or sitting at the window of the bar around the corner, sometimes first thing in the morning, reading the newspapers whilst drinking her coffee.

I have also seen her from time to time in the neighborhood bars, usually stopping only for one drink. "Let's move on. The next bar, let's move on", which is always the cry when bar-hopping in this city. Sometimes she comes into the bars with friends and sometimes alone, and if alone she always end up speaking to someone. From this I would say she was a long term resident in the area. She seems to know everyone or perhaps her gregarious nature, attractive face and infectious laugh make it easy for her to make friends.

She's always smiled at me whenever we see each other on the street or in the bars but we've never spoken more than a friendly bonjour or bonsoir. I've never seen the man before from what I can remember. He's not from around here I don't think although who knows in this city.

"Hello, we booked a table earlier."

The woman says this in perfect English whereas she had spoken in French to me when making the reservation earlier. She isn't drunk but looks as if she's had a few drinks. She looks exuberant, sparkling, and ready to enjoy her evening. I do remember that the man had been standing at the door earlier while she was made the reservation, holding a bottle of what looked like Champagne, so I assume they have finished that before coming here. A few glasses of Champagne always make the eyes sparkle.

"Oui, Mademoiselle. How are you both this evening?"

The man and the woman both smile back at me and say fine, very well, thank you. The restaurant is practically empty but I place them at a table for two near to the bar area, which means I'll easily hear their conversation. I'm not an eavesdropper but it's not busy and frankly I'm bored but also curious about the couple. Maybe more curious about her than him.

I direct them to their seats and hand them both a wine menu.

"French," the man says after a minute, "I know rouge and blanc and that's it. I'm going to have to leave it to you to decide."

"We'll just have the house wine. A bottle of red?"

"Absolutely, that's fine."

I fetch the bottle and open it at the table, pour a little into the glass and wait for the man to taste it.

"That's great. Thank you."

I get the feeling he doesn't have a great deal of wine knowledge but I don't hold it against him. Why should I? It's not obligatory to have a vast knowledge of wine and I try my best to always dispel the falsehood that so many foreigners have of the snotty and rude French waiters. Such a cliché although I can turn it on with some of the customers if needed, especially the foreign finger clickers and the ones who think waiters are mere servants.

The boss took down the sign I had made a few months ago, 'you get the service you deserve' written in English not French. He said it was antagonistic to the customers. If that's the case he should reconsider the décor in here.

The man seems pleasant enough though, friendly but slightly reserved. He still appears nervous, constantly looking around the restaurant and alternating between rubbing his arm and twisting the ring on his finger. Maybe he did a line along with the Champagne. She is relaxed, probably used to eating in restaurants a lot. There are plenty of restaurants in this neighborhood and I know I've seen her in a few.

The only time the man appears not to be nervous is when he is speaking to the woman. He stares straight into her eyes when answering a question or talking to her. His face relaxes as he listens intently to what she has to say. He is quiet, doesn't interrupt her and waits until she has finished talking. A sign, I think, that he trusts her, respects her opinion.
Do they look suited?

They seem to be about the same age. Late thirties I would guess. Both well-dressed although not overly dressed, just casual, understated. They look like a nice couple. I think maybe they would be the type of people I would be friends with, people I would get on with them. What am I talking about I don't even know them.

I would tell the guy to stop looking so nervous for a start. Is he married? Is this an affair and he's nervous of being seen out in public with her? No, I'm not getting that feeling at all from them although I could be wrong. I would say it's still quite an early stage in the relationship. The way they are looking at each other, holding hands over the table, a few weeks maybe, a few nights? I always try to work out these little details before the customers have left the restaurant, it's one of the perks of the job plus I'm a writer and this restaurant is the best place to learn about people's idiosyncrasies and social habits.

Both the man and woman decide to forgo starters and he settles for Beef Wellington, a safe choice for foreigners who are not comfortable with French cuisine. She orders Steamed Mussels in Vermouth. After I have brought both dishes over I return to my listening post behind the desk. For about thirty minutes they discuss the food and where they will go later - nothing much of interest.

"Can I tell you something honest and you won't be mad?" The man says.

Now this sounds interesting. The kitchen staff would have lined up next to me in an instant if they had heard a customer using the words 'honest' and 'won't be mad' in the same question. I knew they were in the early stages of their relationship. I slide my body quietly along behind the desk, closer to them in order to hear clearly.

The woman doesn't put down her cutlery but does stop to stare at the man.

"You're married." She says.

"What? No, no, of course not. I'm not married."

"You're gay."

"No I'm not gay either. Why would you think that after last night?"

"Because that's just the way my luck goes."

She pauses and looks the man directly in the eyes as if she's trying to stare down an oncoming train. "Okay. What is it?"

"It's nothing really, I'm just being stupid. Forget it. It doesn't matter."

"Oh come on, you have to tell me now."

Yes, you must.

"Okay. Well, it's just…this is my idea of hell." He says this as a matter of fact.

"What? What is your idea of hell?" She sounds slightly confused as if she hasn't heard him clearly.

"This. Being in a restaurant. Having people serve me. Being crushed in with all these people."

The woman and I both look around the near deserted restaurant at the same time.

"We're hardly sardines here are we?"

Now she sounds angry. This is a woman with a quick temper if she is pushed.

"No, but you know what I mean."

"No I don't know what you mean. Being in a restaurant, in Paris, with me, eating nice food and drinking delicious wine is your idea of hell? I'd rather you had said you were gay."

"Oh look, come on, I didn't mean being here with you was my idea of hell, not at all. Don't get angry."

The ground should swallow him up right now. My god, what a thing to say. Imbecile.

"Well that's how it sounds to me, how do you expect me to react? Being here with me is your idea of hell. Thank you. Thank you very much. Why not take my head now and push it into your Beef Wellington?"

The woman is furious her face turning red. The man places his hand across the table trying to take her hand but she pushes it away.

"Look I just mean being in restaurants, I'm not all that used to it, it's uncomfortable for me. I don't know why I just always find it hard to relax in restaurants."

"Well you know if you had said that before I had booked this we could have just gone to a pizza place. I would have been happy with a few slices of pizza and a beer. I mean crushed in, what is that? The feeling that you are trapped here with me, that you can't escape or smoke cigarettes when you want?"

Her voice is raised now, in fact she is almost shouting. Shit this is good stuff so early on in the night. Usually the dramatics don't start until much later. I pour myself a glass of red.

"Look, stop. That's not what I meant. We're just getting to know each other and I thought I would tell you something...honest. You said before that I could tell you anything. I'm just not a big lover of restaurants. I'm sorry. I think I picked the wrong time to bring it up."

"You think you picked the wrong time? Really? Remarkable insight for once. Bravo. You came with me earlier to book the restaurant and then you wait until we're having the meal to tell me that this is your idea of hell."

"Stop it." The man says softly but firmly. It doesn't make a difference to the woman's mood.

"It's incredible, I just can't believe it. You are already in trouble with the waiter."

"What?"

What? I had no idea what she was talking about. If anything he was in my good books for the enjoyable theatrics. Shit, what a fool though. I can see what's running through his mind right now - how the hell did I screw this up so badly? The woman has no intention of calming down no matter how many times he asks her to stop or apologizes. To be honest I think she is taking it too personally but it was an incredibly insensitive thing to say. Leave the honesty at home during the beginning of a relationship. There's no need for it, it will only screw things up.

I decide it's time for an intervention before plates are smashed and the entire night is ruined for both of them.

"Is everything alright? Can I get you anything else?"

The woman responds to me in French saying that the food was superb and that she would recommend this restaurant to her friends, and that she writes for magazines and would make sure we were mentioned. I turn to the man who is sitting biting the corner of his lip, one eyebrow raised for some reason.

"Monsieur, do you speak French?"

"No. he doesn't speak French," the woman says with increasing pitch, "he knows nothing of the French, knows nothing of their culture and has no intention of learning I'm sure."

The man sighs in defeat. "Okay, enough. Can I have the cheque please?"

I bring it over to the table and he quickly fishes out his cash.

"Is this enough for a tip?" He asks the woman.

"Yes it's fine." She says whilst putting on her coat and grabbing her bag. "I honestly wouldn't give more than a 15% tip for an evening in hell."

"Bonsoir." I shout as they both get ready to leave and then head to the exit. "See you soon."

They have been in the restaurant for little over an hour.

As they move towards the door I notice that the man no longer seems nervous. Once they have closed the door they both stop and stand outside. Even though it has started to rain they seem in no hurry to move on and I watch them through the glass door, both of them illuminated under the glow of the street lamp.

He says something to her. She looks in the opposite direction, away from his face. He takes out a packet of cigarettes, lights one and gives it to her. Again he speaks and this time she looks directly at him, no longer angry but with an obvious hurt expression. He stops talking and puts his hand to her face for a moment, and then moves his thumb softly across her cheek. At this point four customers push between them barging through the restaurant door, shouting bonsoir at me, obstructing my view of the couple.

When I finally manage to look out again I see only the dark empty street.

Anywhere but Here

How did I get so old in this town?
It was never like this in the city. I never felt old in the city but this town, this fucking town has the ability to suck the sunshine from the sky. This town with its many bridges, bridges that seem to recede the closer you get to them and may as well be brick walls or soundstage backdrops for all the good they do me. These bridges with their illusion of escape make me feel as if a clock is ticking every time I see them. But I can't see them, not from this room.

"When I'm here I don't want to be anywhere else and when I'm not here I want to be here, with you." I answer.

"But you always leave when you could easily stay, and you pick and choose when you visit. I have no say in it. You turn your phone off so that I can't contact you and that makes me feel as if I don't exist."

She's angry although hiding it or more likely getting to the point where she is almost past caring but still cares enough to become angry. In order to show that she's hurt. In order to obtain a response. I ignore seeing the hurt and instead choose to believe that she's just angry, because that's easier to deal with than admitting that I have caused her pain.

"This room really sucks the life out, right? I've never been in a bedroom that didn't have a window. It's hard to be in here. Isn't it?"

"I'm used to it." She turns over on the bed, facing the wall, her back to me. "I've become used to it."

"You should move, really. This can't be good for you. I mean it can't be good for anyone."

"It's not having a window right? That's what it is. Yeah. Right. It's the window."

"I don't know what you want me to do." I laugh as I take another sip of the syrup-like, ice cold vodka.

"Well, I stand here, kind of dancing to the music and you tell me what to do. Work it out genius. Wait, give me some more of that."

She walks over to the bed on which I'm lying. Her high heels clatter as she staggers slightly on the wooden floorboards before bending over to take my glass. I reach out and place a hand on her thigh, run my hand up her leg and under her skirt until she slaps it away.

"Not yet, that's not what happens. You have to wait."

"Okay. Okay. Put the music on and then...I don't know, I'll tell you what to do."

She switches on the music and walks back over in front of the wall of mirrored closet doors. It's dark in the bedroom apart from the candles and the streetlight coming through the window. The music begins and she stands, swaying slightly, the vodka no doubt eliminating any inhibitions. This was new. A suggestion from her to keep things fresh, although I've known her for less than a month.

"Come on, tell me." She says.

"Ah well, take your skirt off. Slowly."

She smiles and begins to unzip her skirt, pushing it down her legs. My eyes alternate between her body and her reflection in the mirror. I stare and take another hit of vodka.

"Okay, okay. I know. Turn round."

She stands facing the mirror, now only in her underwear and high heels. Her eyes or rather the reflection of her eyes look at me. Look at my reflection, looking at her.

"Now bend over." I say. "Lean your head against the mirror and rub your ass with both hands."

She does as I say and I watch her doing this while glancing at her eyes in the mirror as she continues to watch my reflection watching her.

"Now thrust your hips in and out as if you're being fucked from behind."

She starts to push slowly backwards and forwards. I watch from the bed. I watch her ass and then I look again at her reflection in the mirror, her eyes staring at me, her mouth slightly open.

"What now?" She says.

"Now…" I get off the bed and walk towards her.

"No. Not yet. Get back on the bed."

My phone begins to ring.

I ignore it, put my hands on her hips and begin to kiss down her bare back.

Paris isn't a real city, not compared to my city. It's a town, although I seem to be the only one who thinks this. My friends, my new friends since I have arrived here don't agree with my opinion that Paris is too small to be called a city. To me it's a town. Where I come from, now that is a city, a real city.

"You're talking shit, Miles. Paris is one of the most amazing cities in the world. I don't know why you persist with this town nonsense."

"There's something about this place that makes me…" I pour more red from the bottle. "…I don't know what it is but I have this feeling of being trapped. It's those fucking bridges. I want to cross them and keep going."

"Crossing those bridges only takes you to the other side of the city. Stop complaining. You've built a life here. Maybe trying to speak the language more fluently would help. Maybe that is making you feel isolated. Put in some effort."

The restaurant door opens and two women walk in but I'm too distracted to take much notice. I'm still thinking about last night and about how much longer that will last. How much longer until the ultimatum arrives to kill the fun. I don't have to respond to any ultimatum I guess, I could just let it ride, keep it going as it is for as long as possible. In the end it's probably not going to be my decision to make.

One of the women asks the waiter behind the bar if she left a scarf here last night. The waiter mentions something about an argument and the three of them laugh. I can't make out entirely what they are laughing about but I hear the woman say the word 'asshole' while laughing loudly. The two women then sit down and the waiter brings them a bottle of red wine.

"She's nice looking."

"I recognise the one in the green from somewhere." I reply. "I don't know where from though. Maybe she lives around here. Nice looking, definitely, I wouldn't mind."

"Aren't two women enough for you?"

"One woman is more than enough for anyone." I say.

"Only if it's the right woman."

I've been ignoring Ellie's phone calls for almost two days now and I'm no longer listening to the voice messages or reading her texts. I drive down the Quai de la Megisserie past the Pont Neuf and onwards past the Pont Saint-Michel towards the Pont Notre-Dame.

The bridges in this city are tiny. A quick stroll and you're on the other side. It would take at least a fifty minute walk to cross the bridge in my city. Tiny bridges for a tiny town in which I am a tiny inhabitant. If I go back to Ellie's apartment I will become tinier, sitting in a bedroom with no windows. I realise that I am gripping the steering wheel, my fingernails digging deeply into the rubber, pushing the wheel forward with as much force as I can, my jaws clenched together, anger rising inside.

"I don't feel like it tonight. I'm still slightly hungover from last night. I'm surprised you're even working today." Her voice sounds tired or maybe irritated with my request to visit. This is the third time I've called today but the first time she has picked up.

"I wasn't working. I met up with a friend. I've just been driving around. Come on, it'll be fun. You can strip for me again if you want and I won't interrupt this time, I promise."

"Yeah, why don't I believe that? Anyway, what does your girlfriend think of you staying out every night?"

I ignore the question. "I'll bring some vodka tonight."

"No not tonight Miles. Call me tomorrow. I want to go to bed early. Some of us have to work during the day and can't spend our days and nights roaming the streets like some sort of ghostly taxi-driver. I'll call you."

I sit until I've smoked through three cigarettes before turning on the engine and heading north towards the 11th.

"Almost a full two days this time, are you trying for a record?"

"It's been a busy one, Ellie, plus I fell asleep in the car."

"You really think I'm an idiot don't you? It takes five seconds to send a text."

"I'm sorry okay, I'm sorry."

"You mean you're sorry I don't believe your excuses anymore."

I slide under the duvet in the darkness and try to put my arm around Ellie, but she pushes it away and moves closer to the wall, her back to me.

"Why do you come back here? Don't you know this is torture for me? Can't you see that?

Again I move in closer to her and place my arm around her waist, feeling how warm she is, immediately comforted by the familiarity. Again she pushes my arm away.

"Because I don't want to be anywhere else but here."

"But you're never here and you can't stay here any longer."

This is my escape. Being here in this apartment is my escape, even for a short while and I only realise this tonight when I am welcomed through the door. It's an escape from the outside world, from the everyday drudgery of Paris. It's not a real escape in the long-term sense but when I come to this apartment all I have to do is drink vodka, laugh, talk, fuck and for a night my worries disappear. No one knows I'm here and no one can find me here. My mind is free from everything that I cannot stop thinking about outside of this apartment and that is my escape. In this apartment, the outside doesn't exist and the clock stops ticking.

"What are you looking so happy about?"

"Just how much I like being here." I say while pouring two more large vodkas. "It's good. Being here with you is good, you know."

"Well don't get too used to it."

"But we have a good time together, right? We enjoy being with each other. I mean it's not just the sex right?"

"Come on Miles. This really is just about sex. You know that. Talking of which."

She climbs onto the bed and sits on top of me, on my hips and then pulls her t-shirt over her head before throwing it to the floor. I lean over and put my glass down on the bedside table, run my hand across her stomach and look up at her.

"All I'm saying is I like it here. I think, you know, we get on well, we're alike. We have a lot in common. We think alike, that must be a good thing."

"Well, familiarity breeds contempt." She smiles down at me and gives me a look that seems close to patronising before taking another hit from the vodka, shrugging her shoulders and laughing. "You know?"

"You'll change your mind." I say.

"No. I really don't think I will." Again she laughs. I know she's not serious. I start to unhook her bra. And if she is serious I'm sure I can convince her otherwise.

"Wait, no strip tonight?" She asks.

"Do you want to?"

"It's up to you. I mean, if you want to. I'm really not all that bothered."

"I want to but forget the music, it's too distracting."
She gets off the bed and walks over to the wall of mirrors and turns to face me.

"Okay. Let's go."

I'm about to make a suggestion, to tell her what to do when her phone rings. It must be the fourth time it has rang since I've been here and she has screened it every time.

"Why don't you answer or switch it off?"

"I'm ignoring it."

"Who is it?"

"Forget it." She says, looking at the screen before switching it off and returning to her position in front of the mirrors, her back to me. I look at the reflection of her eyes in the mirror as she looks at my reflection and then takes her eyes off mine. "It's no one."

All of Us with Our Pointless Worries and Inconsequential Dramas

"I probably would if I could find a way to kill myself without pain and without causing pain to others."

"So you want to avoid this perceived pain in your life but you won't do it because it would add pain."

"I wouldn't actually do it. I just think about it sometimes. I wouldn't do it because I want to stick around and see what happens, no matter how bad it gets. I mean, doesn't everyone think about it but they don't act on it."

"Some people do act on it."

"Yeah well, some people probably should."

Therapy sessions suck.
I go in there once a week and talk crap while completely avoiding the subject I want to talk about. I could have went in there week one and said that I was having an affair and I felt bad about it and instead of just living with the guilt I had decided to 'get some therapy' along with the rest of my fellow Parisians, the ones who can afford it. I've talked about everything from my shit childhood to my shit job, and now I've reeled out the clichéd suicide card because I think my therapist is actually becoming bored with me.

Last week, mid-session, I saw her eyes glaze over and to catch her attention I told her about the two dogs that I had seen on the way over here that were humping in the street, but were interrupted mid-hump by a man who had come out of his house and poured water over them. Then I told her how I'd like to see that man humping his wife and a dog appearing in his bedroom and pouring water over him and see how he likes it.

I'd really only brought that up during the session because even though she was being paid to listen, she seemed completely disinterested in what I was paying her to listen to. She asked if the image of the dogs disturbed me and I told her no, but it seemed to disturb the man in some way, and he was so disturbed by it that he had decided to disturb the fucking dogs.

Thirty-five minutes into today's session and she had started to play with her executive desk-top sand garden and had only perked up slightly when I mentioned suicide. I shouldn't have brought up suicide because it gave her a glimmer of hope that maybe I did have something for her to solve and when I was saying it aloud I was also imagining her later in the evening googling 'reasons for suicide that I haven't thought of' because she was in fact a terrible therapist and her doctorate was probably from a paid for online course.

Of course this isn't the reality of why she perked up when I mentioned suicide. In reality, she perked up because if I did commit suicide, she would lose a now regular paying client, and executive desk top toys and a summer house in Provence both take heavy financial maintenance.

After my session I meet up with Miles in a bar on Rue Oberkampf. Miles is an expat who's been living in Paris now for around seven years. I've grown bored of this city, as everyone does who has lived in the same place their entire life, but I don't view it with the same contempt as he does, which is strange for such a relative new comer. Maybe if I'd spent years driving a cab every night I'd feel the same way. A rat stuck in a maze with all exits blocked off.

"Therapists are for people with no friends. People with no friends have to pay people to listen to them. They have to pay people to be their friend. You, my friend, are throwing money away."

"Well, you know, she has answers. She can help."

"Not if you don't tell her what the problem is. That's just crazy."

"I can't tell her."

"Then why go in the first place if you had no intention of telling her?"

"I see your point but she might, at a future date, become best friends with my wife, it's entirely possible. They become best friends, they go out for drinks, they get drunk and my wife spews out some family problems, and then at some point during the conversation my therapist says to my wife, 'look, this is confidential and I could probably lose my licence for this but if I don't tell you I'm going to feel so guilty'. So my guilt, which I have unburdened onto her during therapy sessions, leads to her feeling guilty because she now knows my wife, and her needing someplace to unburden this guilt ultimately does not fucking help me in either the short or long term."

"A therapist could have a field day with what goes on in your head. Given your scenario you should have told your wife in the first place and saved yourself time and money."

"Yeah but my scenario has a good chance of never happening."

"My advice, advice which you aren't paying for, tell your wife and come clean or shut the fuck up and live it. You think you're the first husband who has ever fucked around on his wife? There's been a billion before you and there'll be a billion after. And that is how marriages survive."

"She's pushing me to tell her."

"Who?"

"Lillie."

"To tell your wife? Well that's a different matter then and actually that makes things simpler."

"How come?"

"Who can you not live without?"

"I don't think she's that beautiful. I mean me personally, I don't see it."

She had wanted to see the Mona Lisa and it was on her check-list of things to do, a list she'd been working her way through since coming to study in Paris. At 27 years old and fresh off the plane from Algeria, this city was still new and exciting to her. I had met Lillie on a night like any other, in a bar in the 11th, and there was a definite spark, an attraction, which felt, for some reason, as if it were something more.

Talking to her that night I felt something I hadn't felt in years, something I couldn't put my finger on it. Maybe it was simple lust and I was reading much more into it but against my better judgement I agreed to meet her again, to be her unofficial tour guide. Give it a title or an excuse and it becomes simple to ignore the real reason for meeting again.

She didn't mention the ring on my finger until out third meeting, until we had had sex in a hotel room that was inexpensive but comfortable and offered an unhindered view of Montmatre, which isn't quite shitting on my own doorstep but close enough. I was ramping up the Parisian cliché factor and she was giving encouraging signs that she was impressed. In Paris, making love to an almost stranger in a room with a view over the illuminated street tops of the city. Some clichés are timeless for a reason.

Lying in bed in the dimly lit room, my hand resting on her stomach, my wedding ring glinting in the darkness, it was as if I was forcing her to mention it.

She slowly tapped the gold band with her fingernail and said, "So when are you going to tell me about this?"

At some point, during our third month we had met up in the Jardin du Luxembourg on a rainy Wednesday afternoon and strolled through the gardens with no real aim of going anywhere. By this point we just wanted to spend more time together and we had moved from meeting in the hotel room to actually venturing into the city streets. She took my hand in hers as we walked through gardens and I didn't stop her. Although there was the possibility of being seen I didn't want to upset her and I pushed that possibility of discovery from my head.

An hour later we stood in The Louvre with the other tourists, leaning over the railing, gawping at this famous painting. In doing so I felt like a tourist myself or as if I was rediscovering that feeling of showing Paris to my American wife, presenting my city to someone I loved and seeing it again through the eyes of a newcomer, exploring everything this city has to offer with the one person I wanted to be with. Like a thief, I stole some of her excitement and freedom for myself - that feeling of being far from home with all of this time in front of you, in front of us.

"I don't think she's that beautiful. I mean me personally, I don't see it." Lillie mused as we walked along the banks of the river.

"She's different for everyone I guess. Some people look and see beauty, some see the muse and some see the value of that painting only in financial terms. And of course she's timeless, she'll never age. She has proven longevity while others have to contend with their short time on earth and then that's it, it's over. We'll be gone. This, right now, us walking here, it won't even be a memory, but she will still be smiling down at us from that wall."

"Smiling down at all of us with our pointless worries and inconsequential dramas."

That's what Lillie had said in reply to me that day, staring at me intently, a final sentence followed by silence. A silence I didn't fill because I knew what this conversation meant. I knew just by looking at her eyes. We didn't speak again on the walk to the Metro station or when we kissed each other before Lillie boarded her train and I walked on to catch mine.

"Haven't you become everything you despise?"

I listen, hoping that her anger and hatred towards me would be enough of a justification to eradicate the guilt I was feeling. Every hateful comment could help to decrease my guilt down another notch.

"You're an estate agent, don't you hate yourself enough already? Now you're an estate agent who cheats on his wife while he's supposed to be working. You've become such a fucking cliché compared to the person I married. How did this happen? How did I not notice what you were slowly turning into?"

I expected anger. The anger I can handle. It's not as I'm telling her that I've forgotten to buy wine for a dinner party we'd been planning for a week. I'm putting an end to her life as she knows it at this time. I could of course come up with a number of creative excuses about how our marriage was drifting, had been for a long time, and that we both knew we would arrive at this point sooner or later, whether due to a mutual parting of the ways or some other reason of which this is one.

"Why her?"

"I don't know."

"You know. You just don't end five years of marriage without thinking about it. You know."

"I don't know." I sigh. But I do know that nothing I can say is going to make this any less painful for her. "Maybe she has a wrinkle on her face in just the right place and I find it attractive. Maybe she says all of her statements as questions and I find that endearing. Maybe she swallows instead of spits or maybe I was just looking for a way to kill time with someone new over the next five years. The reasons why don't matter."

"Well she's really lucky then. Because I'm pretty sure that she doesn't see your relationship as a way to fill some time. A way to stop the fucking boredom? Are you kidding me?" She pours a glass of wine and drinks half of it. "Does she know you're married?"

"Yes, of course."

"And she just doesn't give a shit right? That's she's breaking up a marriage."

"Something always comes between. It just depends on whether you act on it or not after you've weighed up which you value more."

She stares at me, taking in what I have said. That I now value someone else more than her. She clenches the wine glass and looks at me as I look at her, and then to the wine glass and then back to her face again.

"You think I would?" She holds the glass up higher, reading my mind, as couples who have been together for many years can do. "You'd like that wouldn't you, but I won't give you that. You may be a cliché but I'm certainly not. Leave now and I'll hang a wreath on the door."

"…but I don't really see or hear any actual emotion when you talk about this, about your events, life-changing events that have happened in the past week." She's not looking at me as she says this but continues to look down, moving the tiny rake around the sand, creating a tiny circle and then repeating the motion. "No guilt, no anger, no grief, no remorse, nothing."

"Well, don't worry." I sigh. "When I finally get an emotion, I'll make sure you're the first to know."

Detours

"You always wear those big boots." Esme says as we finally jump into the street after descending five flights of stairs.

"You always wear a permanent frown." I shoot back.

"If it was permanent I would naturally always be wearing it. You messed that up. I'll give you it though. Although I think I have reason..."

"I know." I interrupt, "I know."

"Well at least you dressed up. The suit looks good. We need to get some wine."

"Or Champagne? We can splash out for once."

"Wine will do or we can buy some single malt."

"Single malt, that's a definite. Then we can take it back home and drink it on our own, and avoid this altogether?" I'm sending that idea out quickly although I'm one hundred percent sure of the answer.

"We've talked about this, it's been arranged. We're expected. I have family and these people are now your family whether you like it or not," she smiles, "it's too late to change and you agreed that this is what we would do."

We walk down Rue Oberkampf. The street is empty, not quite deserted but almost, as if Christmas day has arrived seven months early. I cannot believe that some of the shops and bars are still open, although no one is visible behind the illuminated windows. I nod over and smile to a woman riding by on her bicycle, a women I must have seen a thousand times around here but have never spoken a word to. She smiles back. No trouble riding her bike today on the traffic-free streets.

Yes, I don't have any family but Esme's are such a nightmare most of the time that I think I may have gotten off lucky there. Her melodramatic mother, her blowhard brother,

her neurotic sister…but I'm sure things will be different tonight. Of course they'll be different. Esme is the only thing that's important to me anyway. I'm going for her and god knows where I'd be tonight if it wasn't for her.

"Did your take your pill?" I ask.

"No. No, I decided against it."

"Okay. That's good, I guess. I suppose you can always take it later if you change your mind, you still have time."

"I don't think I will."

I light a cigarette.

"You stink of cigarettes."

"Well you," I think for a second or two, I'm grappling here, "stink of yoga."

"Oh that is ludicrous."

But we both laugh.

"Don't light up here."

"Oh come on. Your mother smokes, she won't mind."

"It doesn't look good arriving at the door with a cigarette hanging out of your mouth. Why don't you just open the whisky bottle and have a swig while you're at it." I don't know why she's whispering. If I can barely hear her no-one inside can.

"You're worried about appearances?" I say. She shoots me that look I've seen many times. It's a look I admit I've grown to love and I also admit I've been known to annoy her at times just to achieve that expression. It's a look that a mother gives to a five year old son or daughter, which means 'I'm certainly not going to tell you again'.

"Okay. Okay." I whisper back before returning the cigarette to its packet and ringing the door-bell again. Esme's mother answers, a cigarette in one hand and a glass of something in the other. She puts down the glass on a small marble table next to the door but keeps hold of the cigarette.

"Esme, Esme." She embraces her daughter.

"Mama," Esme exclaims, "you look beautiful. Is this new?"

"I thought I would make the effort. Jacques created it especially. Said I was the only one he would do it for at such short notice, he didn't even charge although…you know I did offer to pay."

"You've given him plenty of business over the years and what's the point in charging you. Is everyone here?"

"Yes, everyone's inside."

Margot finally turns to me, opens her mouth as if to say something but stops and then to my surprise she puts her arms around me, and even more surprising, she kisses me gently on the lips.

She takes a step back and looks me in the eyes, "Thank you." She whispers.

"No, no. We split up about a year ago. You didn't hear? Almost wiped out my bank account."

Esme's brother Tomas, drunk already although it's only around seven, is reminding me, as if I need reminding, that what appears to be a successful life can disappear in an instant, although I don't think anyone has been providing him with much sympathy lately. Of course I had heard about it. He had an affair with a woman who was at least 10 years younger than him. He left his wife and then his lover left him three months later. I had heard he had begged his wife to come back, did all the usual acts of contrition and some highly unusual ones as well from what Esme had told me, but he couldn't buy or talk his way out of this one.

It's not that I can't feel sympathy for him or that I don't understand how he must feel - it's just that he's always been such a dislikeable guy. Conversations with him always centred on money, how much he had, how much his new car or his new set of golf clubs or his new suit or his month long vacation in Monaco cost or how much money he had sunk into his now worthless investments and pension schemes, and I always knew when talking to him that the conversation would eventually lead to how much money I didn't have or that I was wasting my life eking out a meagre existence through my writing.

I had always considered him an asshole and my opinion wasn't going to change simply because his wife had come to the same conclusion.

"Anyway none of it matters now does it?" He says mournfully, pouring another glass of the whisky I had bought. I know that this does matter to him.

"Maybe not, but what does matter now is the people who are here tonight. Those who are here with you now." Sometimes everything I say feels like a cliché. Why did Esme leave me alone with him?

"You were right. You chose the life you wanted, regardless of what anyone else said or thought. I wish I had done that. I wish I could have been so…fearless."

"Is that a compliment I'm hearing? It's been a long time coming. And there's nothing fearless about sticking to one thing because I didn't know or have the desire to do anything else. Come on, you followed love," or more likely your dick, I thought, "that's a brave thing to do, even if it didn't turn out how you thought it would. You still tried."

"I did, didn't I?"

It's something for him to hold on to. I can give him that at least.

"There are lights in here you know." Esme says as she enters the drawing room. "Why are you both sitting hunched up together in the dark?"

I hadn't even noticed that the room is now only illuminated by the almost night sky. I also hadn't noticed that I'd been unconsciously moving the large stool I'm sitting on, edging it away from the shadows creeping into the room. I'd been too lost in my thoughts, as well as listening to Tomas.

"Leave the lights off. Just use candles if you must." Tomas says, taking Esme's hand as she bends down to the table in front of us.

"Have you finished the entire bottle between you?" She holds up the bottle, which was full only two hours earlier. "You're lucky we have more. And don't get drunk, or maybe you should get drunk. I don't know. Maybe we all should just get drunk."

"That gets my vote." I reply.

"Seconded." Shouts Tomas, getting up shakily from his chair and walking to the door. "And thirded, fourthed, whatever."

"You," I say as Esme sits next to me on the stool and takes my hands in hers, "have some messed up family."

"You, definitely fit in well then."

Esme rests her chin on my shoulder and we sit in silence for what seems like a long time.

"I'm at a party in a huge house in the country," Esme whispers into my ear, leaning in closer to me, "and I'm looking for an escape route because I've grown tired of all the people and the embellished stories they tell in order to assuage their fears that they're really not as interesting as they'd like to think they are.

So I leave the party through the huge patio doors and walk outside, down the concrete stairs, away from the lights and the noise and into the darkness of the garden. And before long I find myself wandering along little pathways and past fishponds so still that I can clearly see the moon illuminated on their surface, and on past the hedges that are taller than I am, and I keep walking deeper into the gardens following the moon until I'm so far from the house that the conversations and the music have been replaced by the hooting of owls and a breeze that moves the grass and keeps time with me as a I walk. And I walk further still, until I come to a very old tree, a tree with enormous outstretched limbs underneath which sits a bench, and even though it's raining lightly the bench is dry, sheltered by the tree's branches.

And there I sit, in the warm evening air, in the darkness, accompanied only by the sound of the creaking branches and the music of a thousand droplets of rain falling softly upon the tree's leaves. I sit on the bench alone and I wait."

"For what?"

"For you to come and find me."

I look down to see that the shadows have crept further, almost to the far wall, leaving only one sliver of glowing light trying to outrun the darkness.

I've only been in this dining room once, on my first visit a few years ago, when I was given the grand tour of the apartment followed by a family dinner. It's almost bare in comparison to the other rooms, save for the dining table and chairs, and the shelves along the wall and the two floor lamps. But the lamps haven't been switched on and the room is lit only by three large candles, which sit in the centre of the table, and even the moonlight drifting in through the balcony doors at the far end of the room doesn't reach the corner where we are now sitting.

Small talk. Forced small talk is happening but I'm not listening. I'm looking at the ornaments on one of the shelves. A strange collection of glass and chinaware with no theme to it whatsoever. For a woman who is immaculate and precise in all other areas of her life it looks like Margot has given no thought at all to this collection of small cats, china plates, music boxes and tacky-looking holiday souvenirs. And in the centre of all of this disarray sits a large glass elephant, facing directly forwards towards the dining table. The only piece on the shelf that looks as if it has been placed deliberately.

I look over at Margot and realise that she's been watching me as I look at the ornaments, and it looks as if she is about to say something but she then turns her head back to the shelf and then slowly back to me, and she smiles. I'm not completely sure what she has shared with me in that moment but she puts down her empty glass and announces to the table, "I'd like to say a prayer before we start eating."

"Oh come on mother," Tomas, who is sitting to her left, says loudly, "none of us here are religious. You know this."

"You don't have to join me. I'm not asking for that."

"You should have gone to Notre Dame with the rest of them then." He retorts. A sneer in his voice, slurring his words slightly.

"Just give me this can't you. One prayer. Just one!"

"Let her say her prayer Tomas. What difference does it make?"

This is the most I have heard Esme's sister, Adele, say all night apart from our first greeting. She's sitting directly opposite me and it's only now for the first time that I notice how much she resembles Esme. The same long, dark hair and brown eyes. The same caramel colour to her skin and the slightly turned down mouth that can make her look unhappy even when she's not, although I haven't seen her smile in a long a time. But Adele has a slight scar running down her forehead, about three inches in length and which you can only see if her hair is tied back. Plus Adele worries about everything. Esme is a worrier but not nearly to the same level as her sister. I wish I had asked Esme how Adele had received that scar.

Margot finishes her prayer and then gives thanks that we're all here tonight.

"I can't remember the last time we were all sitting together like this but I'm glad we are." Says Adele.

"I can." Tomas replies while filling everyone's glass again.

I can remember as well and I hope he has it wrong or that he thinks more about what he is about to say and doesn't say it.

"When you were pregnant remember? And we had that dinner to celebrate."

Adele looks stunned as if she has had her breath stolen from her, "That's right. That was it. I forgot. I mean…"

"Well, I don't how you can forget that, come on it…"

"Do shut-up Tomas and put your phone away for once." Margot cuts him off.

"Idiot." Esme hisses at him. She takes her hand off mine and reaches over to hold Adele's hand.

"I'm sorry. Look I, I didn't think. You know what I'm like. I'm sorry Adele, I'm sorry." He is almost pleading with her. I can imagine this is the same way he pleaded with his wife, who he's no doubt hoping is going to text or call him tonight, which is the reason he has barely let go of his phone all evening. After all this time, a year later, still hoping.

"It's okay. It doesn't matter. It was a long time ago. I just forgot with everything going on. Although, no, it has been on my mind for the past few months, now and again but it's not important."

But even in the candlelight, with her head bowed, I can see the tear running down her face. And although I want to stop seeing that tear, to turn around and look out through the balcony windows, I don't.

"It is important," Margot says, "and you shouldn't forget. None of us should."

The half-empty plates remain on the table long after the meal is over. None of us has had much of an appetite it seems but we are all drinking the wine and the scotch, and the nervous, subdued conversation is now no longer a problem. Esme has decided to tell the story of the drunk woman we had met outside a bar a few weeks ago.

"…and she was sitting there on the ground, so drunk, I mean incredibly drunk and we are just standing around her smoking cigarettes, and she keeps saying something but neither of us can make out what it is. And then suddenly she raises her arm in the air as if she's asking a question and Michael, the idiot, bends down and slaps her hand with his, gives her a high five." Esme has told this story a few times and each time she finds it hilarious for some reason. "And the woman looks stunned and then shouts at Michael that she's asking to be picked up not given a bloody high five."

Everyone begins to laugh.

Esme's mother, who I have never seen laugh this much or even much at all, shouts out over the table, "I'm glad I never went swimming at the beach with you, Michael."

"A few days ago I saw a man walk in front of a car. Straight into the road. Straight into the traffic."

"Was he drunk?" Tomas asks.

"At first I thought he was because his face was emotionless, glazed over," Adele replies, "the way he just walked casually out into the road but the cars stopped for him and he continued to the other side. But then, instead of walking on, he turned round again and he walked out into the traffic, and he kept doing this again and again."

"Did anyone hit him?" I ask.

"I don't know. I just drove past him. No one was helping him and no one stopped him. When I looked in my rear view mirror he had turned his back and he was walking deliberately into the oncoming cars."

"With what's going on in the world today I don't blame him at all." Says Tomas while pouring another glassful of whisky. We've all had plenty to drink but the drunkenness has gone now and I don't think it's going to return no matter how much we try to recapture it.

I wonder what Margot and Esme are talking about. Margot had said she wanted to speak to each of us alone. They've been gone for about half an hour now. I look at my watch and calculate that there's not enough time to spend half an hour with each of us, I don't think, but I know, or at least I think I know, that Esme has always been Margot's favourite, even though parents aren't supposed to favour one child over another. But that's usually the case.

Esme finally returns and I can see she has been crying.

"She wants to see both of you together."

They both stand up and look at their older sister who says that it's okay, that there's still time, and they walk slowly out of the room.

"Does she want to speak to me?" I ask as she sits down next to me.

"No, she said you would understand and she would only be telling you what you already know."

The candles have almost died out, the flames flickering but still holding on. I want to ask Esme if she is scared but her reply, if it's a yes, will only make me more scared and I don't want that but I can feel my heart racing as I lift the half-empty bottle that's at my feet and drink from it to try to extinguish the fear. I drink a large amount of the whisky and pass it to Esme who drinks from the bottle, her arm tightly around my waist, and as I look at her as she drinks I wished that we were anywhere else but here. She puts the bottle down and rests her head on my shoulder.

"Tell me again." I say.

The room is almost in complete darkness by the time Margot, Adele and Tomas return. There's only the moonlight to guide us now.

"Well, it's time." Says Margot quietly.

I take Esme's hand and we all walk towards the balcony doors and I push the handle down but then stop before opening the door.

"Now?"

Margot looks at me and nods.

A soon as I open the thickly glazed doors I hear the screaming and shouting coming from the streets beneath us. The illuminated city appears in front of us as we step out onto the balcony, and I take a deep breath of the cold night air. I put my arm around Esme, pull her tightly against me but there's nothing I can do to stop her shaking, and I steady myself, steady both of us by placing one hand on the balcony railing.

Tomas stands drinking from a bottle, muttering something again and again but I can't make out what he is saying. Adele is holding onto Margot who is motionless, staring up into the night sky, but then both of them back away from the railing until they reach the glass doors and slowly slide down until they are seated, their arms around each other.

Esme tries to say something but her shaking has become worse and the noise has become so loud that I begin to feel light-headed, and I'm finding it hard to breathe but I'm sure I can hear her saying, "you…". And although I don't want to turn my head from her to confront the black sky, I do.

And I see the hundreds of dots, glowing and becoming larger. Dwarfing the tiny stars behind them.

Relationships

Strangers

I'm standing in a doorway. Two people are standing in front of me, a man and a woman. They look as if they are maybe in their late twenties. I'm trying to get my bearings having just woken up and I realise that I must have fallen asleep in a doorway standing up.

"Hey you alright?" The girl asks me.

"He's wasted man, look at him."

"Shut up. He's awake." The girl replies.

"Yeah, I'm, yeah, I'm okay."

have no idea whatsoever how I got here. I have no memory of leaving the pub at all last night and no idea where I am. I still feel half-drunk but at least it's dark out so I know I haven't slept here all night.

"Shit where am I?"

"Tooting man. You live here?"

"No, shit, I live in Wandsworth. I need to get a taxi."

"Hey," the guy asks, "you wanna' split some money for some weed? I know where I can get some."

This is all sounding too familiar but alcohol always brings bravado and a joint sounded good right now. I search through my pockets and find some notes.

"Here's twenty. Where do we need to go?"

"Nah, it's okay, I'll be back soon. You stay with Chantelle." He shouts, sprinting down the deserted street and disappearing around the corner.

"Well that's the last you'll see of that money."

"What?"

"He ain't coming back with that I guarantee it. Do you always just hand out money so easily?"

"Aw you are kidding me?"

"No," she laughs, "I know him, he's gone."

"Great. The perfect ending to another non-memorable evening."

"I feel bad for you now. I spotted you standing there and wanted to make sure you were alright. He's harmless, you don't give him money though. I know that much."

She smiles at me with a face full of pity. Chantelle, if that is her real name, is very pretty with a stunning figure clad in a skin tight dress and at least she seems to have a conscience, which would have been a more helpful attribute if she had said something before I had given her friend the money.

"Look, I feel bad. How about we share a taxi to your place and I'll pay for it okay?"

"Do you live in Wandsworth?"

"No, I live in Elephant and Castle, but you know we could keep each other company for a while, be a laugh, I've got nothing better to do. Do you have any drink at home?"

"A bottle of wine, that's about it."

"Fine, come on. You should at least get something for your twenty pounds."

"I don't need to buy company you know."

"Twenty pounds would not buy my company believe me." For some reason I did believe that. "But I'll give you some credit. There's a taxi, come on."

I open the bottle of red and pour two glasses. Chantelle is sitting on the floor going through the films next to the television. I have to admit her body from this angle is enticing and just as that thought enters my head so does last night and Jade. What had happened? I check my mobile for messages but there's nothing from her. I'm not calling to find out. I'll wait until she gets back to me, if she even does get back in touch with me.

"Some good ones here. You want to watch something?" Chantelle asks.

"Not right now."

I hand her the glass of wine.

"You got any weed?" She asks.

"Well I would have if your friend had come through on his promise. How do you know him?"

"He's my pimp, sometimes anyway."

"What?"

"Yeah I'm a prostitute. I'm gonna' die soon you know. I've got a disease."

She makes these three statements in the same way someone else would say they were going to the shops for a pint of milk.

"Look," she says before downing the glass of wine in one and the pouring herself another, "I don't want any funny stuff okay. I know I came back here with you but nothing's going to happen, alright?"

It suddenly dawns on me what is happening. I don't believe the prostitute stuff for a minute. She is simply protecting herself making sure nothing happens to her and what better way than to do that than say she has a life threatening sexual disease, although in reality that's no guarantee of protection.

"Chantelle, you have nothing to worry about. I'm not going to try anything okay. You're free to leave whenever you want. Do I look like the kind of person who is going to hurt you?"

"There are some fucked up people out there. You can never be certain just by looking at a person, I know this through experience. Do you live here alone?"

"Now I do. I had a flat mate but she left to go back home."

"Can we watch a film?"

"How old are you, Chantelle?"

"23."

"You should really be more careful than to just end up in a stranger's house you know."

"Okay, thanks dad."

She seems to relax. The defensive element has now gone from her eyes.

"Choose what you want to watch, I don't mind." I say lying back on the sofa.

Whatever her problems are I am too tired to go into any big discussions. She seems troubled, and I can tell by the way she is now onto her third glass of wine to my one that she is one of those people who won't stop drinking until they have passed out. But who am I to judge? She puts on the film, staggering a little as she walks back from the television, and then sits, gazing contentedly at the screen as I drift off to sleep.

For the second time of the night it takes me a few minutes after wakening to remember exactly what has happened, and then, unfortunately, I do remember. The television is on, the empty wine bottle is lying on the floor but there's no Chantelle lying asleep on the sofa. I walk through to the bedroom but she hasn't crashed out on the bed either. The bathroom door is closed. I try the handle, locked.

"Chantelle, are you okay?"

No reply.

"Chantelle?" I say louder, knocking on the door.

Nothing. She is either in there asleep or…or what? Looking over at the sofa she had been sitting on I spot a knife. That hadn't been there before. She had obviously decided she needed some protection while she slept.

"Chantelle, can you open up please?"

I bang on the door again, try to kick the lock in, still nothing, complete silence. She wouldn't try anything like that, would she? How the fuck do I know? I don't know this girl. I don't know what she's been through. She could be a completely depressed drug addict for all I know. Another kick to the door. This is the cheapest plywood door I've ever seen, how is it managing to hold up to my kicks? I need something to wedge it open.

I find a large screwdriver and jam it into the door frame. A few hefty shoves and it finally starts to budge. One more push and the frame cracks open, and I shove the door in and there she is, lying completely passed out on the toilet floor. How can she possibly sleep through all this noise? I bend down and rub her face gently.

"Chantelle? Chantelle are you okay?"

Nothing.

She is out cold and as I place my arms underneath her and lift her up I realise that she weighs next to nothing. I carry her through to the bedroom and lay her on the bed. Taking off her dress isn't an option, especially as she will have no memory of what happened the previous night and I don't want her to freak out when she wakes up in the morning. I simply pull the duvet over her, shut the curtains and leave her to sleep it off.

Lying back on the futon I light a cigarette and stare at the roof as the early morning light starts to filter through the curtains.
Should I worry about these situations I keep finding myself in? Am I attracting these damaged characters or are they attracted to me? Jade isn't damaged, not that I can see, so why didn't I end up spending the night with her? Why is having a few drinks, alright more than a few, resulting in me ending up in these situations? Memory loss means I am having blackouts, doesn't it?

This can't go on. Something has to change.

"Would you like some soup?"

Chantelle is standing over me. She seems wide awake and oblivious to last night's mini-drama, and for some reason she's talking about soup.

"Soup?" I say, staring at her face, which looks as good this morning as it did last night whereas I no doubt look like the proverbial bag of shit.

"Yes I thought I would make some soup for breakfast."

"Do I even have any soup?"

"Everyone has soup, don't they?"

"I doubt I do and anyway I can't face anything at this time of the morning except caffeine and nicotine."

"Morning? It has gone noon you know." She laughs and then pauses. "I can't really remember going to bed last night but thanks for letting me sleep there."

I decide not to tell her about the passing out in the toilet scenario. I hate it when people remind me of drunken incidents and really I don't want to embarrass her.

"Ah, that's okay. I'm used to sleeping through here anyway. You were really tired so I said you could use the bed."

"You mean I managed to walk to the bed? I felt kinda' sick when I woke up, which isn't usually a good sign for me. I didn't do anything bad did I?"

She seems to be looking for embarrassing tales as if she were used to them but I can't actually be bothered with a big conversation.

"No, no you were fine. You just watched a film. My memory is pretty hazy as it is, so I'm not a reliable witness."

She looks at me for a moment, stares, as if searching my face for an answer then turns away.

"Okay, tres bon." She says brightly. "We could always go to the pub for a drink."

"Oh god no, I have to work today so the pub is out."
I lie.

Really, I could do with some more sleep and just the thought of alcohol is making me queasy, and I have a definite acid stomach burn thing going on. She seems friendly enough but the thought of having her sitting in my flat for another few hours is something I can do without.

"You want me to go don't you?" She says, her voice now turning slightly downbeat. "That's okay really I understand."

"I have to work that's all. It's nothing to do with you being here." Lies again and to make it even more obvious I'm not actually looking at her as I speak.

"Is it okay if I at least make coffee?"

"Yes of course, there's no hurry."

She walks through to the kitchen, which is located right next to the bathroom, and I watch as she stops still for a second and looks at the broken bathroom door frame, but then she simply moves on through to the kitchen. I doubt she can remember anything that happened once she passed out in the bathroom, but it's no big deal.

Just a typical Saturday night.

Drinking coffee on a Sunday morning with a beautiful woman is not my idea of hell. But this hangover is starting to seriously kick in and I just want to climb back into bed. It's been an hour now and Chantelle still doesn't seem in a hurry to go anywhere. She has already suggested the pub twice and asked if she could watch another film, both of which I have declined. Okay, so it's time to drop the subtle routine.

"Woh, it's getting late. If I don't start work soon I'll be up all night. I need to go to the shops first to get cigarettes before I start so…I'll walk you out."

Chantelle sits there staring at me and then smiles.

"I'm not an idiot Cal. You want rid of me, it's okay I'll go. Don't you like having me here? I mean, you are on your own, don't you like having company?"

Fuck, she's one of these people who will call you on something and forget about social boundaries and not making a fuss. I thought the English were experts at being polite and taking a hint?

"Chantelle, it's great having you here, honestly. What's not to like about you? But I have to work."

I'm now starting to realise that I am following a route of lie. Lies designed to get this girl out of my flat. She is actually telling the truth and being honest with no pretences. How does this end up becoming so difficult?

"Mmm, did I say something stupid last night?" Again she is searching for answers. "Sometimes if I'm drunk I will say stupid things but don't take them seriously. I know I drink too much and I've been told before that I can get a bit obnoxious when drunk."

"No don't worry about it, really. I'm the last person to say anything about anyone's drinking. Remember how we met last night? Really it's fine."

"Well okay but I'd rather people were truthful and honest with me. Too many liars in this world and I've dealt with my fair share of the bad ones, and I know now how to protect myself."

I remember the knife by the sofa as she says this. Chantelle looks at my face and laughs.

"You have a million different expressions you know that? Talk about wearing your emotions all over your face. You'd be

useless at poker. Okay I'm going to get a taxi home. I couldn't borrow ten pounds from you could I? I've got some money but just not enough to get back home."
Typical.

Thirty minutes later after managing to obtain my phone number and saying that she would call during the week, and after a kiss on the mouth beside the taxi outside my flat, Chantelle is gone. I feel some sort of relief just not sure what kind. She wasn't really that much trouble and anyone can fall asleep on the bathroom floor after drinking too much. If I hadn't felt the need to smash in the bathroom door she would have just woken up on her own and I wouldn't now have to fix the bloody door. Still, she has friends who take money from strangers and then disappear with it. Who needs that in their life?

I make my way back up the narrow stairway to my top floor flat. On the way up my elderly downstairs neighbour's door opens and her head peaks out.

"Noisy, noisy last night." She says this but there is no anger in her voice.

"Yeah sorry about that Myra was a bit of a late one. Hope it didn't keep you awake."

"Be more careful. I see you kissing outside. Be more careful."

"I will, don't worry. Too much drink that's all. Have a good one, Myra."

She shuts the door and I proceed up to the flat. Myra, nice old woman, hasn't left her flat in twenty years. I only got to know her because a package was sent to her flat instead of mine. Never usually hear a peep from her. Twenty years inside a flat, alone in one of the largest cities in the world.

Many people would call her sad but maybe she has simply created a world in which she can exist and be herself without the need of the drama created by others. It's a brave person who can live such a simple and contended life. I guess it all comes down to perspective. Perhaps I will nickname her Buddha.

Running with the Bulls

"It feels different this time, don't you think?"

I look up from my newspaper to Serena, who is standing washing dishes with her back to me. I know what she is referring to. She says exactly the same thing every time we get back together after a break up.

"You say this every time."

"But it does, it feels different. Better than before. More permanent."

To Serena we are now, once again, on the honeymoon period and everything is perfect. The honeymoon period can be relived again and again after every break up and make-up. Our entire relationship now seems to be based on this cycle and I'm starting to debate whether Serena needs either the pain of the break-up or the happiness of getting back together in order to make our relationship work for her. Getting back together, where our need for each other seems more intense than before - does she see this as a reassurance of our love for each other?

I don't reply to her question and continue to read the article about running with the bulls in Pamplona. The sunlight is streaming into the small kitchen, the golden colour illuminating the room. It's Saturday morning and the whole weekend stretches ahead. Maybe she's right. Maybe it will be different this time. It feels good to be back with Serena and I'm looking forward to spending the weekend with her.

"I'd like to try that, running with the bulls." I say.

Serena sits down at the table and picks up her coffee cup with both hands. She blows on the coffee and then takes a small sip. She's wearing a thick, black jumper with a high neck. Her black fringe hangs down across her forehead and frames her small, dark face. Her eyes always look permanently confused and hurt, always seemingly watchful for anything that may cause her pain.

"Actually it's called running of the bulls and I think it's sick." She says. "They kill the bulls at the end you know. It's cruelty to animals and you say you want to take part?"

"No. I don't agree with killing bulls, of course not. I'm just saying it must be pretty exciting. The atmosphere, the crowds. It's a test of endurance, a battle of wills."

"Well I don't think it is fun for the bull." She slams her coffee down. "It's barbaric, inhumane and you want to take part in order to prove how masculine you are. Killing a bull for an exciting experience."

"Oh Jesus, don't get so angry. I'm just saying it would be interesting. It's not like it's going to happen. It was a comment and you have to blow it up as usual."

She gets up from her seat, throws her cup into the sink and now this can go either way. A simple argument could end either with me walking out or her telling me to get out of the house. If either scenario occurs it will mean that I would not return, or be allowed to return, for days or even weeks. Stubbornness is a defining trait that we both have in common. I decide, for once, to simply leave the room for a while in order to calm down.

Lying on the bed I hear crashing dishes and then silence. I switch on the CD player and Simon and Garfunkel starts playing The Only Living Boy in New York. The bed I am lying on is, without doubt, the most comfortable bed I have ever lain on. It is an old double bed given to Serena by her father when she moved into this flat. I had loved the feeling of it from the first moment I had sprawled out on it. The softness, the warmth and when Serena lay with me on it, a feeling of safety.

In the early days of our relationship we used to meet every Tuesday morning at her flat. Tuesday mornings were just for the two of us and all activity was centered on the bed. The curtains would be drawn with the only light in the room coming from the small table lamp. Her flat was situated in a quiet area of town, no traffic going by and the only noise that could be heard was the occasional bird song outside of the window.

    In the dark room we would eat breakfast together on the bed, read newspapers or simply talk about our lives before we had known each other. It seems impossible now to think of a time without Serena. It's as if she has always been with me and I can't imagine a future without her. Back then, Tuesday mornings were for lying under the quilt together, feeling her warm breath, kissing every part of her, laughing at jokes that only the two us would understand if we said them in the presence of others. Always just the two of us. It was as if we were children who had taken a morning off from the world in order to hide and play.

    Those mornings would eventually stretch to around three in the afternoon and every week they seemed to get longer and longer, and it was always an effort to get out of bed and not be able to touch Serena's skin anymore. When I eventually moved into Serena's flat, Tuesday mornings gradually became no different from any other day of the week.

I sit up on my elbow and look at the bedroom door. I can hear two people in the kitchen talking and whispering, and then the bedroom door slowly opens. It is not Serena but her eight year old daughter, Lucy. She walks over to the bed holding a piece of paper. As she silently hands me the paper it strikes me how much she looks like a miniature version of her mother, the same hurt, confused eyes. And then she turns and leaves the room.

I unfold the paper and shakily, in felt pen, Lucy has written the words, "Please stop fighting." Above the words there is a drawing of a child with a sad face. I sit and stare at the note and my stomach sinks as I think to myself that those words, written by a child, should be enough to permanently end any arguments.

When I enter the kitchen, Serena is sitting reading at the table. I sit down next to her and take her hand in mine.

"She has more sense than us." She says.

"I know."

There is silence for a few moments as we look at each other.

"Serena, we need to stop fighting over every little thing. I love that you are passionate about things but we are not against each other. We just had a childish argument about bull fighting."

She laughs softly while pushing her hair from her forehead and then kisses me gently.

"I was thinking in the bedroom," I say, "about when we used to meet on Tuesday mornings. I loved those times. I cannot remember the last time we had a Tuesday morning together."

"Those were nice times. I wish every day were like those Tuesday mornings."

"Well we can't every day. I mean I would never get any work done for a start." I say, looking at the newspaper lying on the table, still open at the picture of the running bulls trying instinctively but hopelessly to escape their fate.

"We need to keep the excitement for each other alive ourselves. We will find ways, we always do," says Serena, standing up, "it's going to be different this time, you'll see."

Serena lets go of my hand and walks to the kitchen sink where she rinses the coffee cups.

"But we can keep excitement alive without all these arguments and dramas?" I intended it as a statement, but it comes as a question.

Lucy comes skipping into the kitchen and begins tugging on her mother's jumper, swinging her arm back and forth.

Serena places a hand on her daughter's head while staring absently out of the window.

"Perhaps." She replies, as the colour gold once again enters through the kitchen window.

The Conversationalists

She is not the type of woman who will look back on her life with regret over the men she has left behind.

When she dumped me it was quick and painless, for her, while I was left to work out which of the 3000 reasons in my head was the most valid for her disappearance. It's not like I didn't have a life before she arrived and she didn't magically appear out of nowhere to give my life some meaning. I was doing fine before she arrived or at least it seemed that way at the time.

And I tried to fight off any type of relationship at the beginning because even a friendship at that time seemed like an inconvenience. But she was persistent, and it began and it continued even though I knew from the start that eventually she would leave without thinking twice and continue on without looking back.

She was beautiful and had a personality that I couldn't deal with, maybe because it was a personality I had never encountered before. It was the personality of all about me and there's nothing wrong with that, we all want to talk about ourselves.

Sometimes she would arrive unexpectedly and then sit and have a six hour conversation. I timed it once. Actually I timed it by the fact that it was midday when she arrived and it was dark outside by the time she had finished talking. It wasn't really a conversation, it was as if I were watching a hologram of a person sitting on a sofa, speaking continually, giving a detailed monologue of how their week had went - not the highlights, not the most interesting parts but every detail.

I would sink slowly into the armchair, melting into it, the force and continuation of her words and sentences and stories eventually sucking the life out of me, the exact same words, sentences and stories I had heard only the week before, and yet for some reason I was powerless to end it. And as her conversation continued, chapter upon chapter, my mind began to question the reality of the situation.

After the second hour my inner voice began saying, "This has to stop soon, she's bound to run out of steam. No one can talk for this length without pausing."

By the fourth hour that voice was pleading with me, "Make this stop for the love of god. Why are you just sitting here listening? Actually you're not even listening anymore, you're just nodding along when she pauses. I don't think you've actually said anything in two hours. Your eyes are dead."

By the fifth hour I tried to make a run for it but she followed me into the kitchen. As I spooned the tuna fish into a pan she asked why I was eating cat food and then said, "Well as I was saying" and continued.

When hour six eventually arrived my face looked like a coat that had seen better days, a coat that someone had decided to leave at the back of the bus because it was beyond repair. I could barely move from the chair. I was exhausted, mentally and physically drained, she had water-boarded me with words.

"She's just lonely. She's just arrived. She doesn't know anyone else in this city. Give her a break."

"She cooks you dinner once a week. Is it too much to ask to listen to her thoughts for a few hours? Be a friend to her."

"She's maybe on anti-depressants. That's what happens when people are on anti-depressants. They can talk continually after being in a coma like state for days."

After one year exactly, she disappeared from the city and moved on yet again. Her last conversation with me included the statement that she was leaving and had no reason to return to this city.

Although I think about her from time to time and about those conversations, I have never heard from her since.

Kryptonite

Things had been going great and then one night she announced that she wanted a cat. As soon as she had said it, that cat was already in the room and I knew what was coming but I gave it a hopeless shot anyway.

"It's out of the question, I'm allergic to cats. My ex, she had a cat. I used to wake up and it would be sitting on my head and I'd be unable to breathe."

"We can keep it out of the bedroom. This is my house and I don't ask for much else." She looked out of the corner of her eye at me as she said this. Not much but always something else.

The cat wasn't mentioned again and two weeks later we split over an argument that probably had a hidden subtext but was, on the whole, inconsequential.

Within a week we were back together and when I entered the house I saw the cat curled up on the sofa. It eyed me for a second and then looked away as if it had already risen above me, as if it is was saying prophetically, I was here before you and I'll be here once you're gone. Cats are wise or so I've heard.

"Ah the cat has arrived."

The cat was allowed free reign of the house and it never went outside. Why would it? Everything it had was right here. It shit in a tray in the kitchen and sometimes slept on the bed, the same bed that we slept in. I took some anti-allergy pills but they didn't make much of a difference.

When the cat was near me for any prolonged period of time I became breathless, my eyes watered, my skin itched. And that cat always seemed to be near. When I noticed the cat was on the bed I usually threw it out of the room, with some force at times but as soon as the bedroom door opened a couple of inches it would run back in and jump on the bed.

One night I awoke, gasping for air. It felt like I was breathing through a straw. I looked up from the pillow and saw the cat lying across me.
"The damn cat is on the bed again, I can't breathe."
"Okay, okay, hold on."
I lay there waiting on her throwing the cat out of the room but instead she leaned over me and opened the window an inch.
"That's not going to do any good."
"The air will help you breathe."
"Jesus Christ. When superman is dying because he is lying next to a lump of kryptonite do you think Lois Lane opens the fucking window?"
"Superman?"
The cat lowered its head and went back to sleep.

The next day the cat had vanished. The window in the bedroom had been left wide open and it appeared to me that it had wanted to experience life on the outside. I had been called in as part of the search committee. That cat could stay lost as far I was concerned. If it was never found it would mean I had a better chance of not dying in my sleep. But I could see the worry on my girlfriend's face, she was even considering putting up 'reward for lost cat' posters around the neighbourhood. It had only been gone an hour.

So I trailed the streets looking for a cat that I didn't hate but wouldn't be altogether unhappy if I never saw again. People on the street looked at me as if were crazy when I shouted out its name, repeating the same word over and over again. I was looking for a cat but to everyone else I was simply a guy wandering the streets shouting out the word Monkey. I doubted this cat even knew that its name was Monkey and if it did, it wasn't the sort who would accept that as its name.

I made sure not to look at anyone directly when shouting out the cat's name.

After searching for a few hours I went back to find that the cat had returned. It had been hiding under some bins only a few feet from the house. The big wide world had been too terrifying and it was back, settled in nicely on the bed, recovering from the trauma of leaping from a window and hiding under some bins. The cat raised its head an inch, looked me over dismissively and then went back to sleep.

It's no doubt still there on that bed, content with its life.

The Route

I truly hated this paper route.
It hated it but I knew that suffering this route was the price I would have to pay until someone else gave up one of the better routes, the ones in the areas where you were actually given tips from the customers. The customers on this route didn't tip, ever.

This paper route, my first one, was in an area that was considered a poor part of town. It wasn't that the area was that bad just that it had a reputation of being bad and I wasn't too sure where that reputation came from. All I knew was that no one else wanted this route and it was always given to the new starts.

"Start at the bottom and work your way up. Pay your dues." Said the boss. "Keep at it and you'll get one of the better routes, eventually."

Eventually.

Every night after school I delivered the newspapers, walking along the long crescent stretch of tenement blocks that seemed to go on for at least a mile. Small flats piled one on top of the other, five high. In these tenement blocks you were only a foot up, down and sideways from your neighbour. This was the outskirts of town and if you walked behind the tenements you would see only fields stretching out into the distance. Five nights a week I would walk up and down the dark stairwells, smelling the cooking from behind the doors, hearing people shouting at each other, babies crying, dogs barking, televisions blaring, every night the same.

Mondays to Thursdays weren't too bad, I didn't have to see the customers but I dreaded Fridays because on a Friday I turned from someone who delivered the nightly news into a bill collector. Very few of the fifty or so customers I tried to collect from would answer their door when I arrived on a Friday night. A handful paid their bills on time but others would tell me to come back next week, they would pay double next week or triple the week after that, but most just simply didn't answer the door. Some people hadn't paid their bill in months and of course to the boss it wasn't their fault that they hadn't paid, it was my fault that I hadn't collected.

Once the unpaid bill crept up to three months the boss would say to me, "Get the money this week or tell them they are cut off, no more papers."

Why didn't he tell them this? I'm only the person who delivers the news. I knew this area, I knew these people. They *were* the type to shoot the messenger. I had to pay my dues by trying to collect from people who didn't want to pay theirs.

It's true that this paper route was a pain the arse but there were events that added some colour and while I delivered the news I also heard the news.

There was the couple who argued almost every night, "I know you've been out drinking, I can smell it on your breath." Shouted the woman from behind the door.

"Oh for Christ's sake, this again? That's from last night. I didn't brush my teeth today." The man shouted back, hopelessly pleading innocence.

A week later as I was pushing the newspaper slowly through the same letterbox, I bumped into the presumed guilty man with the alleged beer breath. He opened the door slowly and quietly, removing the newspaper softly from the letterbox.

He whispered to me. "I'll take that and good luck trying to collect the bill from her kid."

I watched him walk quickly down the stairs, almost running, newspaper in one hand, suitcase in the other.

I stood at another door and listened as a woman shouted at a man, asking why he had flushed the goldfish down the toilet, to which the man shouted back, "Because I felt like it alright. I just felt like it."

There was the girl who followed me around every night and would hand me love notes every now and again. I told her that instead of giving me love notes she should get her mother to pay her newspaper bill once in a while. She did of course tell her mother and when I went to collect the bill I was told to keep my big yap shut to her daughter about her financial affairs. She still didn't pay her bill although she now probably felt justified in not paying due to my indiscretion and I learned a valuable lesson about knowing when to keep my mouth shut.

And then there was the man with the dog.
It wasn't his dog, it was a stray dog that used to follow me around occasionally. I never used to let the dog into the tenements but one night it snuck in behind me, probably looking for some warmth. I went up the stairs to deliver newspapers and when I came down a shirtless man was standing at his door looking at the dog.

"Is that your dog?" He asked, not looking in my direction, just staring intently at the dog.

For a moment I hesitated, wondering why he wanted to know and then I answered, "No, not mine."

The man disappeared behind the door for an instant and then returned holding a hammer. He brought the hammer up above his head and then lunged at the dog's head but that dog was skinny and quick, and the hammer connected only with air and then the concrete floor with a bang that echoed up the empty stairwells. The dog sprinted to the tenement door, which I opened and we both ran out of.

Something different happened on that route every night and there were times when sitting bored at my school desk that I actually found myself looking forward to the characters and events that would take place on my nightly visit to that street. But the dog incident stayed with me and no matter how hard I tried I just couldn't understand what had made the man want to hurt the dog.

The dog incident was one of the reasons I asked my boss every night if a new route was coming up.

"Soon, soon." Was always the reply. "Everyone…"

"…has to pay their dues." I sighed.

"Now you're learning."

Fridays weren't just about collecting the bills. Fridays also meant watching the drunks. Friday was pay-day and for the working men it meant a morning at work and an afternoon in the pub before heading home to the wife and kids. Most would just stagger home, eyes glazed with nothing else on their mind except making it to bed but now and again it would happen.

Now and again I would see a drunk guy playing with the cars. They would slowly walk along the pavement, sometimes staggering or weaving but when they came to the road they would straighten up and walk calmly across without looking. Any oncoming cars would be forced to brake suddenly but the drunks didn't acknowledge what had happened, they would simply keep on walking while the driver swore or shouted or sat there behind the wheel, shaking, having almost run someone over.

I wasn't sure if this was a death wish or a battle of wills between man and something bigger, something unstoppable. Maybe it was a test of manhood or simply a desperate last bid attempt not to go home but in this game, with the drink providing Dutch courage, the drunk guy always won.

Eventually I moved to a paper route in a better area, one that I knew well because I actually lived on the street where I delivered the nightly news. This street had houses with well-maintained gardens in which well-fed dogs with collars chewed on bones and jumped up happily whenever they saw me. People paid their bills on time every Friday and I actually made more in tips than my weekly wage.

    I had paid my dues and finally had the easy route with the easy money and someone else would be climbing those dark tenement stairs hoping to be next in line for the job I was now doing.

    My new route was less than a 10 minute walk from my previous one but in all honesty, in all the time I delivered the news on the new route, nothing eventful ever happened.

Recorded Delivery

Every couple of months my uncle would send me some stamps. They would arrive through the letterbox in small brown envelopes.

I don't know why he did this, I had never met him but someone must have told him that I had started to collect stamps. My uncle was in the merchant navy, travelling to different parts of the world and yet when the envelope appeared it would be filled only with British stamps, always the same kind. Whenever the envelope arrived I would open it and out would fall 10 or 20 British stamps.

"Why are they always British? Why doesn't he send me stamps from all these places he goes to? There's no point having a stamp collection if every stamp is exactly the same. He should just stop sending them." I thought to myself.

Not wanting to seem ungrateful I didn't tell anyone or complain about my growing pile of stamps.

These deliveries from abroad went on for about two years.
Over the course of the two years I naturally became bored with stamp collecting and moved onto exploring nearby and sometimes not so nearby towns on my new bicycle.
And still the stamps came.

One day another envelope from my uncle appeared. I ripped it open and of course another pile of British stamps fell out. I didn't know it at the time but this was to be the last envelope from my uncle. That day, I sat against the door and began turning the envelope over and over in my hand, imaging all of the far away countries he must visited and all of those envelopes he had sent me full of stamps taken from letters that had been written to him from many other people or perhaps just one person.

Yet he never wrote to me when he sent the stamps, never placed as much as a note inside the envelope.
All he did was send me the stamps.

All he did, this uncle I had never met, was to take the time to collect these stamps and send them to me every couple of months, without fail, from wherever he was.

My uncle finally stopped sending me the stamps when he left the merchant navy and returned home.

If I was smarter at that age than perhaps I am now, I would have realised that on the front of every envelope I had ripped open and discarded, sat a shiny foreign stamp.

I would also have realised, as I do now, decades later, that the stamps were not really the point.

Grand Canyon

It didn't creep up on him unnoticed as it had for others who found themselves in this situation. Isolation isn't generally welcomed as a lifestyle choice for most and usually only comes to people in the later years when friends have dwindled and family visits grow less regular due to commitments or travelling distance or other unoriginal excuses. This wasn't the case for Burdon Warwick, who could still, at 33, be regarded a young man.

Seclusion, isolation, living a life within only the walls of his house was an actual choice, one that he had imposed and one that he came to enjoy when he eventually realised that he had not left his home in years and had no intention of doing so anytime soon.

Not many people could afford to live like this, thought Burdon, they probably wished they could live as I do. This wasn't an excuse or a justification he used to convince others that he actually liked living this way. Burdon had no need to convince others because in his world, there were no others. And it wasn't as if Burdon lacked intelligence. Due to his abiding passion for self-analysis he was fully aware of why he had chosen to cut himself off from the rest of the world. He knew exactly the root of what others, if there had been any others, would likely call his 'condition'.

When Burdon was 13 years old a three week family vacation to the Grand Canyon had been planned. Unfortunately, only a few days before the trip was due to take place, he had contracted mumps. The child watched from his window with a burning combination of almost unbearable anger and sadness as his father, mother and two brothers, Sven and Humphrey, jumped into the gleaming new pick-up truck with the rented jet-ski strapped to the back.

There was going to be no trip to see one of the wonders of the world for Burdon. No jet-skiing on the world famous lakes and no sight-seeing in Colorado. All of the activities, which the family had planned together in detail for what had seemed like months, were now lost to Burdon. Instead, the boy was confined to the house with his elderly aunt who had arrived with board games, knitting, a copy of the TV Guide and a constant need for sleep.

A week later, his father arrived home alone with news of the incident that would indelibly stain the rest of Burdon's life.

The family had been picnicking near the edge of the canyon one morning with the intention of heading off to a nearby lake to use the jet-ski. When it came time to leave for the lake Burdon's mother cleared the picnic items and then began arranging the boys for a family photograph while Burdon's father went back to the truck to fetch the camera. His father had faithfully promised Burdon more than once that he would take plenty of family photos during the trip.

Once in the truck Burdon's father thought it would be an idea to drive forward a little. As he recounted the story later to his son who had asked why he had started the truck, Burdon's father said he had no idea why he had chosen to do this. It may have been because he wanted to point the vehicle in the direction they were to be going or to warm up the engine, he simply couldn't remember. What he could remember was the heavy thump as the front wheels of the truck slid into a hole and the sharp sound of something snapping, as if a tightly wound steel cable had been cut.

He had then placed his foot on the accelerator to push the truck forward and out of the dip in the ground. The truck lurched upwards, to the left and quickly forward. In that same moment Burdon's father heard the deafening screech of metal and then silence.

When Burdon's father got out of the truck he found himself alone, staring at the panoramic view of the Grand Canyon and the immense canvas of blue sky. For a second, he had said, he couldn't comprehend what was going on, as if his family were playing some incredibly well thought out joke on him. Both the jet-ski and his family were gone.

"I knew what had happened, I knew immediately" said Burdon's father, "I just didn't want to believe it."

Burdon's father had sat beside the edge of the canyon for the rest of the day, through the night and for much of the following day before he eventually sought help.

"It was you Burdon." He said to the boy. "When I remembered you I knew I had to move."

What Burdon remembered most about that time and what stuck in his mind as if he had heard it only yesterday was a comment made at the wake after the funeral. As he wandered from room to room among the family mourners and friends, trying to find a space away from the people that he did not know and did not care about, and who did not pay much attention to him except to give a pitying smile when he passed by, he overheard two men talking, discussing the accident.

He recognised these men as salesmen, work colleagues of his father and standing next to the men he watched as one took a bite out of a sandwich. Large slivers of grey shredded beef fell from the sandwich onto the floor as the man spoke, "To call it majorly unlucky would be an understatement."

The other man, who was having trouble supressing his laughter, downed his drink and replied, "You got that right. I guess you could call it a tragic boating accident at the Grand Canyon."

By the time he had reached the age of 18, just after the death of his father, Burdon had not only become financially independent but independent of anyone. The money from his father's will and the sale of the house was more than enough to tide him over for a few years without employment. This wasn't however, to be the end of the increase in Burdon's finances.

Ironically, for a man who now did not communicate much with anyone, Burdon had made a killing from an investment in an internet start-up company that specialised in social networking. When his money had grown to the point where he felt safe enough, Burdon began making plans.

By the age of 30 Burdon had removed himself as far as he could from his home town in the U.S. He bought a large house on a large island in Europe, a beachfront property that overlooked sand dunes that were, from what he had read in the sales blurb, of unique scientific importance and of unparalleled, breath-taking beauty. When he had arrived at the house he was surprised to find that for once, the photographs and clichéd text in the sales brochure weren't lying.

From his large front window he was greeted each day with an immense sky of ever changing colours and miles of golden sand dunes that stretched to a cliff before plunging dramatically to another beach and the sea. Every morning and every evening he would stand at the window to witness the sunrise and sunset as another day began and disappeared. Sometimes he would stand at the window for hours watching the colours of the sky and sea change minute by minute. This is a place, thought Burdon, where seasons actually exist.

At first the changing seasons unsettled him. He didn't want to be reminded of time ticking by. He wanted, at best, a perpetual similarity, a place where things did not change. In the end, Burdon recognised that the seasonal calendar was a small price to pay to live in a dream of his own making. The illusion of control was enough.

It was the delivery man who alerted Burdon as to how others in the nearby village viewed him and to a disturbing fact – one he had never, no matter how much self-analysis he had undertaken, considered.

On the last Saturday of every month Burdon would receive his groceries from the village supermarket. His online order never varied and all that was required to receive the groceries was the simple click of a button. Burdon paid his bill online and had sent an email to the store informing them to leave the groceries at the door. For years this system had worked. There was no need to make small talk with the delivery man and no need to have any other interaction in this process other than the click of a button each month.

Today, however, the grocery man lingered at the door, as if waiting for something. When Burdon approached the door he saw the man's blurry body through the frosted glass panel, peering in, his hands against the glass. When Burdon was less than a foot from the door the man knocked loudly against the glass.

"Are you there?"

Burdon remained silent, unsure of whether or not to make his presence known.

"I can see you," shouted the man, "I know you're there."

Why is he encroaching on my life? The rules have been set out, this shouldn't be happening, thought Burdon.

"Things are happening, big things." Shouted the blurry figure through the glass. "You need to be aware of what is going on."

Burdon forced himself to speak. "Just leave the groceries and go. I don't want any trouble. I don't need to…"

"You are there." The man said quietly with a hint of surprise. "Look, I know you don't like to be bothered by people but we need to talk? It's important. I have a message. I have information that pertains to you. This is affecting everyone."

By now, both Burdon and the man were less than 10 inches apart, separated only by the thin, frosted glass.

What could a grocery man tell him that would be of such importance?

"I'd like you to go please, just leave."

"Not until I have told you what is going on."

This isn't right, thought Burdon as he backed away from the door. There are rules. I don't have to deal with this.

"Just leave the groceries and go. I'm not continuing this conversation."

"It will only take a few minutes, please. This affects you." Shouted the man.

Burdon retreated from the door, silently walking backwards, his entire body tense, his jaws clenched.

The man dropped his hands from the glass and turned to the side but didn't walk away. Another figure appeared at the door.

"Is he there?" Said a second man.

"He's not going to discuss it."

"Did you tell him what's going to happen?"

"I think he's gone back inside."

Burdon stopped and listened as the two men continued to talk.

"Look, just leave the leaflet. There's nothing more we can do. He's a recluse. We knew this wouldn't be easy."

The first man placed his hands against the glass again, "I'm leaving a note for you Mr Warwick, this is important. You need to get in touch with us. You're the only one left who doesn't know. There's an email address on the leaflet. Please just read it."

Burdon didn't answer. He simply stood and watched the two men through the glass.

"Come on, I'm not standing here forever." The second man said loudly. "He won't be able to stay a recluse anyway, not for much longer."

"Maybe once he reads the leaflet he'll get in touch."

"I wouldn't bank on it." Said the second man as he moved from the step, still talking loudly, making sure Burdon would hear if he were still listening. "His type care only about themselves and then end up dying alone, so what? Why should we care if he can't be bothered to even talk to us? Come on, let's go."

The first man stood at the door for a moment, sighed and then turned to go but then turned back and spoke quietly through the glass to Burdon.

"Just read the leaflet Mr Warwick. I don't think there is much you can do but you need to be aware of what is going on. None of us will be here much longer."

It was at least an hour after this encounter that Burdon forced himself to move from where he was standing in order to retrieve his groceries. He wasn't standing there for an hour to make sure the men were gone, he was standing there trying to make sense of the words he had heard the second man use – recluse and dying alone.

Obviously he did fit the actual definition of the word recluse but he had never thought of himself in such terms. This was now, he understood, how the world or at least how the people in the village saw him but did this mean he was actually a recluse?

I can only be a recluse, thought Burden, in relation to other people but if there are no other people in my life then how can I be a recluse? I am only a recluse to them and it's only when they have had some contact with me that can they call me a recluse. If they had no contact with me they would not know me or anything about me and could not call me a recluse. If they have had contact with me then obviously I cannot be a recluse.

This line of thought ran through Burdon's mind until he had exhausted all possible permutations, until he had satisfied himself that the word recluse would bother him no longer and was a label that did not apply to him.

Dying alone, however, was something that Burdon could not come up with a satisfactory explanation to or to why the thought of what this man had said had irritated him. This had never bothered him before because he had never thought about it before in relation to himself.

What difference does it make to the delivery man if I die alone? There's no shame in dying, alone or otherwise. Why did he hurl this at me as if it were an insult, something to be ashamed of? And what does it matter if all I do is think of myself? Am I bothering anyone else with my life?

These thoughts spiralled in Burdon's mind to the point where he became frustrated to such a level that he punched the wall in front of him with enough force to make a sizeable hole in the grey plaster. The blood from his wounded hand flecked the edges of the hole, and wiping the wall with the cuff of his shirt only resulted in encrusting the blood stain deeper into the paintwork instead of eradicating it.

The leaflet from the village lay on the marble sideboard for two days before Burdon decided to read it. He had resisted throwing the leaflet into the garbage and instead placed it on the sideboard next to the window at which he stood each day. For those two days he would glimpse the leaflet from the corner of his eye, picking up slightly more information each time he looked down. At first he could just make out the image on the cover, the image of a beach, the very beach he stared at each day.

This has nothing to do with me, thought Burdon as his gaze moved from the leaflet back to the beach, back to his beach.

Intermittently, throughout the two days, Burdon slowly pieced together the information from the front of the leaflet as if completing a jigsaw – the image of the beach and then the words 'Thurrock Enterprises' in red letters across the top of the golden sand dunes in the photograph.

Finally, Burdon picked up and began to fully read the leaflet after making out the words 'Luxury Golf Complex' just above the photograph of the beach.

It had been years since Burdon had actually used the internet for anything other than paying bills and shopping online, and as he typed the name Donovan Thurrock into the search engine he felt that familiar pressure on his chest, the anxiety rising once again as it had years ago whenever he connected with the outside world through this small portal that had in the past spewed out nothing but bad news.

Donovan Thurrock's image appeared on the screen, a mountain of man with what looked like some sort of impossibly high, rigid hair and glowing ruddy cheeks. In the picture, Thurrock stood on stairs leading up to the entrance of a private jet plane, the words Thurrock Enterprises emblazoned in huge red capital letters across the body of the plane, his arms outstretched above his head as if he were either being welcomed triumphantly or was setting off on a journey of some importance and saying farewell to an adoring multitude.

During the next five hours Burdon learned all he needed to know about Donovan Thurrock, a business man who had, it seemed, little originality but plenty of money to build hotels around the world, and now he was coming here, to Burdon's home, to build a golf course, a luxury golf course.

What is the difference, Burdon thought, between a golf course and a luxury golf course apart from the fact that adding the word luxury means you can charge more money to use it. It doesn't matter to me that a supposed better class of people are coming here in their ludicrous, brightly coloured clown-like clothes to play their imbecilic game. What matters to me is that these people are coming here, to my beach, to a beach that will no doubt no longer exist, people that I will see and hear every day from the moment I stand at my window, there will be no escape.

The implications of what was actually about to happen, how his life was about to irrevocably change were still not fully apparent to Burdon.

To Donovan Thurrock, Burdon was an inconvenience at best and a nuisance at worst. To Thurrock, Burdon's property and the surrounding beach were little more than markers on a board game. Unbeknownst to Burdon, his property had no future whatsoever. Thurrock's plan was to eradicate it from the landscape to make way for a hotel, a luxury hotel.

At approximately the same time as Burdon was uncovering details that the golf complex had escalated from the planning to building stage Thurrock was making deals with local leaders, smoothing the way, greasing the palms and making promises of regeneration that looked good on paper but were little more than velvet soaked in snake oil.

Nothing was going to stop Donovan Thurrock, not the many protests that had already taken place against him or the fact that he was about to destroy an area renowned for its beauty and historical importance. To Thurrock, he was creating history not destroying it and as Burdon's anxiety increased with each new discovery of the fate of the beach, Thurrock was adding a final touch to ensure nothing could stand in his way – the compulsory purchase of all beachfront properties.

"I understand that you are dismayed regarding the purchase of your property and I do sympathise but a fair price has been agreed upon. Our company has tried repeatedly to reach you regarding the sale prior to the compulsory purchase but to no avail. Mr Warwick, I will let the strong language and threats in your previous email pass as I know that you feel under pressure and apprehensive about leaving your home but I hope you understand my position and can at least be grateful that I am being more than generous with regards to this purchase, which will go ahead even if it means eviction. I hope it will not come to that and I hope that you can enjoy your last remaining days in your property.

As you know the work has now started and I'm sorry Mr Warwick but there is nothing that can be done to stop progress. I intend this to be one of the best golf courses in the world, in fact I don't intend it to be – it will be, and you alone cannot stop this."

You alone cannot stop this.

Thurrock's words became a mantra in Burdon's head. You alone cannot stop this. He reread the email, picking out phrases and words that he thought Thurrock had deliberately written to humiliate him, to make him feel powerless. Thurrock was allowing him to enjoy the remaining days in his property, that progress could not be stopped, that he understood and sympathised over the pressure Burdon was under but that *he alone could not stop this*. Again and again he read the email, his frustration growing that there was nothing that could be done to stop this, that one man had the power to obliterate his life, to obliterate a landscape completely, quickly and with little effort or thought to others.

That he alone could not stop this.

Over the next few days Burdon sent Thurrock continuous emails, each one growing increasingly abusive. He criticised Thurrock for his unoriginality in business and the smallness of his mind due to a severe lack vision and imagination when it came to his business ventures, that he was a cancer of a man to be pitied rather than looked up due to his tiresome pursuit of money and his gargantuan ego. Burdon called Thurrock a vandal, a miscreant, a large man with small ideas and compared him to someone setting fire to priceless works of art in order to collect on the insurance.

On reading the stream of emails, a new one arriving approximately every two hours, Thurrock was at first amused at the meanderings of this mad man. He was more than used to dealing with such irritants and had easily disposed of many protestors and obstacles throughout his business career. Money was usually the answer to any problem that came his way and if that didn't work there always more money and if more money didn't work, well, this was business, and if he couldn't buy them off then he simply bought those who could help to eradicate his problems.

But as the emails continued and the abuse grew, Thurrock began to simmer, turning the words of scorn over and over, and he then began to take slight satisfaction in imagining what he could do to Burdon. While sitting at his desk he pictured himself arriving at Burdon's property, grabbing him by the neck, kicking him out of the door and off of the land while providing no mercy as Burdon begged for forgiveness.

Who was this man, this recluse he had been told, too scared to do anything with his life, who simply existed, who thought so little of the money he had been offered. Who was he to feel superior, above him enough to insult him professionally and personally, to call him a man of little imagination who was laughed at by those with real ideas and creativity? Now it was Thurrock who reread the emails and burned as the insults hit home, dug into his skin and inflamed deeply hidden nerves.

Burdon eyed the clock again as he paced his living room.
In little over an hour Thurrock would arrive at Burdon's home. The voice in his head was constant, intermittently changing mid-thought from a pep talk to an inner howl of desperation and fear.

Keep it together, you can do this, thought Burdon. This isn't me, this is not how I live my life. How has it come to this. I cannot do this.

For the last two weeks, since agreeing to meet with Thurrock, he had thought of little else.

Why am I doing this, he had asked himself, I can leave again. This needn't be a problem.

The overwhelming impulse to give up and leave would only be quelled by looking out of his window towards the huge industrial machinery that was now being used to flatten the dunes. Although he had not yet left his home the work on the complex had begun. Each time Burdon's electricity and water supply was interrupted due to the work, each time one of the huge diggers plunged its jaws into the ground, eating the beach, he felt a wave of anxiety that was soon replaced with anger, an anger that only made him more determined to stay on the path he had chosen.

As each new day brought the disappearance of another piece of Burdon's land another email was sent to Thurrock.

Thurrock filled Burdon's doorway, obliterating the early evening sunshine trying to push in behind him. In the flesh he appeared even larger than Burdon had imagined from the photographs.

"Thank you for finally answering the door Mr Warwick. For a moment there I thought we weren't going to get the chance to meet." Thurrock said, holding out his huge hand to Burdon who ignored the gesture and simply replied, "We?"

Another man appeared as Thurrock inched his way through the door. He was smaller and younger than Thurrock but wearing the same pristine black suit and overcoat as worn by Thurrock.

"This is my son. He's overseeing the completion of the work on the complex. You can call him Junior."

Without even acknowledging this introduction Burdon turned his back, walked along the corridor and disappeared into the living room.

"Should we go in?" Said Junior.

"Son, we own this place." Thurrock said calmly as he began to walk down the corridor and into Burdon's home.

Thurrock found Burdon standing by the window, looking out at what was left of the beach.

"You're progressing as planned?" Asked Burdon without turning round to face Thurrock.

"Progressing? Yep, we're on schedule and we're…"

"Sorry," Burdon interrupted as he turned around, "I didn't mean to say progress I meant to say destoying."

"Really Mr Warwick, can I call you Burdon?" He continued without waiting for an answer, "I know your feelings on this. I've heard exactly what you think over the last month and it's too late now, it's over. Your position has been noted but it's time for you to move on, as everyone else has."

"I don't want to move on. This is my home."

"It was your home. It's mine now, my land and soon to be my hotel."

"Once you've demolished it."

"Yes, if you want to talk frankly, yes, once I've demolished it."

Thurrock sat down and took a bottle of whisky from the plastic bag he had been carrying.

"Why are you here Mr Thurrock? What exactly is it you want from me, you have everything."

"Call me Donovan," Said Thurrock opening the bottle. "Junior can you fetch me some glasses? I'm here because I want to at least try to set the record straight between us, to make you see that I'm not the ogre you've painted me out to be. I'm just a man, a business man looking to do some good, to create something that can be enjoyed for generations to come. I don't usually do this, in fact, after reading your emails I was of a mind to simply have you thrown out of this property as quickly as possible."

"I convinced him otherwise." Said Junior handing the glasses to Thurrock. "My father can have a temper sometimes and you certainly got under his skin."

Thurrock shot his son a look of disproval, "Thank you Junior. But you can understand, I'm sure Burdon, that the things you said, in the emails, would irritate me slightly and they did yes, slightly at first but I understand. Here, have a drink."

"Thank you no, and please, do feel free to call me Mr Warwick."

Thurrock sighed, stood up and walked to the window, standing beside Burdon. "That's going to be giant sand pit by the edge of the cliff. The view here is, well, phenomenal." He said, looking into the distance at the immense hole in the ground that lay beside the edge of the cliff.

"Amazing," Burdon replied, turning to face Thurrock. "How do you think these things up? Do you have a committee?"

"I know you think I'm a man little imagination."

"It's not a thought Thurrock, it's a fact."

"Well Burdon," he emphasised Burdon's name as if sneering at it, "I'm out there creating. I live in the real world and it's men like me who make this world what it is. Once you've made any sort of mark in the world you will realise what that means."

"You call a golf course creating? You call destroying a place with this much beauty making your mark? You are an imbecile Thurrock. You are what is wrong with this world. This is about money and your inflated ego and nothing else. You are as fake as these frankly ludicrous boots you are wearing."

Thurrock looked down at the red alligator skin cowboy boots and then back to Burdon. He was about to say something then stopped, pursed his lips, clenched his jaws, took another drink, sighed and sat back down.

"Junior," Thurrock said calmly, "could you get the present for Mr Warwick from the car."

As Junior left the room Thurrock poured himself another drink and stared at Burdon's back.

"I've come up against people like you before and usually they are far more powerful than you Warwick. What you seem to fail to realise is that you," he said calmly, "are insignificant, you are spec. You are a fly that I've already squashed and you don't have sense enough to die."

Burdon turned to face Thurrock. "I pity you, as a huge number of people out there do, but you, Thurrock, don't have sense enough to see it. Aggression and attack, that's all you know but to most people you are simply a ridiculous excuse for a human being."

Thurrock shot up from his chair, his face reddening, staring directly at Burdon.

"What?" said Burdon raising his voice, daring Thurrock, "what are you going to do? You know you seemed much larger when you first came here but now I can see that you are very small Thurrock, a tiny man. Maybe those boots help you to be appear larger."

Thurrock took a step towards Burdon.

Junior entered the room with a large bag strapped over his shoulder. "Here it is. I have his present."

He stopped as the two men faced each other. "Is everything okay here?"

"Everything's fine Junior, fine." Thurrock said, breaking eye contact with Burdon. "Mr Warwick and I were just having a little heart to heart. Airing our differences. I was setting him straight so to speak. It's fine. Give me the present now."

Junior handed the long red, leather bag to his father who turned to face Burdon.

"Now Burdon, this is just a little token," he said with a smile, "something to remember me by. I hope you'll appreciate it. Do you play?"

Thurrock took the leather cover from the top of the bag to reveal a set of golf clubs.

"No."

"That's a shame, you should consider learning. Maybe there'll be a golf course near your new home. A great many deals have been made on golf courses. It'll open up a whole new way of life for you. Out in the sunshine, the fresh air, the great outdoors, nothing better."

He stood with his hands on top of the clubs, silent, staring, waiting on Burdon's reply. The only sound in the room was the tapping of his red leather boots on the wooden floorboards.

"Really?" said Burdon with a sigh, "this is the best you've got? I take it back Thurrock, to call you an imbecile would be to denigrate imbeciles. You are the imbecile's imbecile. How many months did it take you to understand the rules of golf? You can leave now."

Burdon walked past Thurrock, not looking at him, out to the corridor, out to the front door. As he opened the door he felt the cool air on his face and narrowed his eyes against the bright sunshine. He stopped for a moment, unsure, his heart beating rapidly but then forced himself to walk out of the doorway and onto the dunes.

Thurrock's heart was also beating rapidly. His fists clenched, the anger rising up inside as he watched from the window as Burdon strode across the sand, past the diggers and stood by the edge of the sand pit.

"This guy is unbelievable Dad. Why are you letting him to talk to you this way?" Said Junior.

"Shut up." Thurrock replied, staring out of the window, drinking his 40 year old whisky.

"Let's just get some of the security guys and throw him out now. You've already allowed him to stay longer than he should."

"I told you to shut up. You think I can't deal with people like him?"

"You don't have to deal with him, that's the point. You've already won here."

Thurrock watched from the window as Burdon stood with his back to him in the distance, not moving, simply standing by the edge of the pit, his hands in his pockets. He then licked his lips and downed the dregs of his whisky.

"I'm going to take the first drive on this course."

He grabbed a club and ball from the bag and walked out of the room.

Junior poured a glass of whisky and stood by the window. He hated this business, he hated his father's theatrics, his bullying business methods, his childish temper tantrums and stubbornness.

He can be a world class asshole, Junior thought, but there's nothing much that can be done once he sets mind on something.

He watched as his father strode out in front of the house and pushed the tee into the soft ground, gently placing the ball on top before taking a few practice swings. Apart from business, golf was his father's passion and he spent most of his free time on courses around the world. This game had always seemed like a complete waste to time to Junior.

Grown men playing games, he thought, grown men.

Junior walked over to the now half empty bottle of whisky and poured himself another drink. He took a sip and walked back to the window to see his father striding purposefully across the sand, the golf club still in his hand, walking towards where Burdon would have been standing except that he could now no longer see Burdon.

"I shouted fore. I gave the warning, I shouted."
Thurrock was bent over, lightly slapping Burdon's face, trying to revive him.
"What did you Dad? Aim right at him?"
"I shouted fore, this isn't my fault. It's not my fault if he doesn't have the sense to move."
"Is he even alive?"
Thurrock continued slapping Burdon's face.
"Yeah I think so, more's the pity." He said looking around the apparently deserted area, checking for witnesses. "If he were dead we could have just thrown him in the sand pit, buried him, it would be like he never existed."
Junior turned and ran back towards the house.
"I'm going to get the whisky, maybe that will help revive him."
"Yeah you do that." Thurrock said. "You do that."
Burdon lay on the sand, listening. He listened to Thurrock's breathing, felt the sting from Thurrock's hands as he slapped his face, smelt the whisky, but still didn't open his eyes. Thurrock lifted Burdon's head, cradled it in his arms and began to talk in a calm steady voice.
"You know the problem with you Warwick? You've never had to struggle, never had to fight for anything, never tried to do anything with your life but you still think you have some sort of right to have your say against people like me. I'm a creator Warwick and you, you're nothing.

I know you can hear me, I know this is sinking in to your pathetic little head. Here's a lesson from someone who actually matters. People need something to fight for, to fight against and I provide that, I understand that, and I'm happy with my role. But people like you, who have went through their entire lives without something to fight for or against, you simply end up fighting yourself, and that always makes my job a hell of a lot easier."

Burdon felt Thurrock stand up but still made no attempt to open his eyes. He remained still even as Thurrock began pulling him into a sitting position.

"You decided to fight once the game was over." Whispered Thurrock as he slid the body of the golf club under Burdon's neck.

"I told you that you alone could not stop this," he continued, as he used the shaft of the club to pull Burdon up by the neck and into a standing position, balancing Burdon's body against his and then slowly moving forward until Burdon was hanging freely over the side of the pit, suspended by the club under his neck, "and you never could."

As the cold steel pressed deeply against his throat, Burdon Warwick opened his eyes, instinctively raising his arms to grab the club, to stop Thurrock's stranglehold. But almost immediately Burdon stopped struggling, let his arms fall and listened, not to Thurrock, but to the sound of the wind and the waves crashing on the beach below.

Lowering his eyes he looked out over the beach below him, the beach that would now never change. And Burdon smiled as the sun sparkled and grew brighter against the immense canvas of blue sky.

The Urban Jungle

Note to readers

I can relate to people who say that they feel as if real life is happening elsewhere. I've lived in London three times now and the last time, for around five years, was the longest. My relationship with that city is definitely a love and hate thing, the type of relationship a lot of people have with their cities. London was never boring although sometimes the jobs I did were extremely tedious and were all mostly just a way to survive financially, and they all involved a lot of time-killing, especially when I was a temp worker. But that city did have a sense of community, a feeling as if you were all part of something, a shared struggle if you will, to make it through another day.

But I moved on from the London period and wrote about it in the novel Leaving London. The working title of that book was *London: an Unrequited Love Story,* which not only summed up my feeling about the city but also about certain people I met and developed relationships with while living there. Leaving London is basically a love story and not all love stories, as we know, are happy ones, although there may be some unforgettably happy experiences along the way. But to get back to the point of my first line in this note – whenever I'm away from the city I feel as if life is happening elsewhere. As if the city is calling out to me, saying, "Where are you? Why aren't you here? You're dying there."

The stories in this section are mostly taken from the novel but certain stories such as *Filter Image,* never made it into the book and were simply the beginnings of my writing about my experiences in the city. *The Last Busker in London* was a story that was found online by an editor who paid me to place it on her new citizen journalism website and this made me think that maybe a book was the way to go. *The End of the*

Nineties was the original story, (although never published in that form), the theme of the book and that storyline makes up the backbone of Leaving London.

Leaving London is, I would say, around two thirds fact but people have been changed, locations are different and of course fictional characters and storylines exist throughout. Leaving London may be gritty, dark and depressing but I hope the humour comes through because a city, or rather the people who live in a city, need and use humour to help them get through each and every day.

If I had to sum up Leaving London in one sentence I would use a line from Milan Kundera's novel, The Unbearable Lightness of Being - *"Pick me up," is the message of a person who keeps falling. Tomas kept picking her up, patiently."*

How to Be Depressed in London

London is a great city to be depressed in.
In London there are plenty of things to see and lots of angry people to argue with over the slightest little thing, which will momentarily take your mind of your problems. And the great thing about London is that it already has lots of depressed people, it's teeming with them. You can't pop a valium without tripping over an extremely morose homeless person or a depressed office worker. Depression in London has become an epidemic and really there should be some sort of congestion charge for this sort of thing.

Being depressed in London could be a themed vacation and for a writer it's heaven. If the powers that be were smart enough they would make a killing from charging a fee in order to allow people the enjoyment of being depressed in London for a while. Another great thing is that if you are depressed in London other depressed people will naturally gravitate towards you; misery loves company.

I had moved to London after breaking up with a long term girlfriend. We had moved from Scotland to a small town in England just outside of London, a town that had the highest rate of senior citizens and over 80s in the UK. This meant we had moved to a town where there was a good chance that people would be decomposing right in front of our eyes as we talked to them,; good choice! My girlfriend announced she was leaving after I had returned from a holiday in Spain. Actually she didn't announce it she just wasn't there when I got back. Fair enough, I deserved it. I promptly became depressed, which was actually more of a long-term feeling sorry for myself kind of state.

To add to the misery she took the television and left me with a radio. A radio that seemed to constantly play the song The Drugs Don't Work by The Verve every time I switched it on, which was the number one song at the time I think. This song played even once is enough to place coma patients into a depressive state let alone people who have just been kicked to the curb. It was as if the DJ was just waiting on me getting up from the floor, yes the floor, where I lay for about a week, and switching on the radio before shouting in that excited, annoying, dog humping a couch DJ way, "AND NOW THE VERVE."

The Drugs Don't Work – a song that will drive anyone who listens to it enough times to ingest enough drugs to prove that The Verve were wrong and that the drugs actually do work. Thus I moved from the graveyard capital of the UK to London.

Moving in with the Indian stoner probably wasn't the smartest move. She had also undergone a break-up and was as depressed as I was. Weekends would go by in a blur, we couldn't even remember which films we had just finished watching. Most of our conversations would end and start with, "what were we just talking about?"

Her favourite pastime was to come in from work, sit on the couch, light up a joint and say, "analyze me." This meant I had to ask her a series of psychiatric type questions pertaining to her break up. She would then give me one of many vague situations or arguments leading to her break-up and I would come up with an overall assessment of why this reason added to her boyfriend walking out and why she was feeling the way she was. Secretly, I had my money on the pot smoking before, during and after work as well as the constant lava lamp gazing and tarot card sessions as just a few of the reasons for the boyfriend's exit.

I got so good at the analysing she thought I had some sort of psychic ability. Basically, there's no secret to it – if you have been dumped by someone and then you are analysing why someone else has been dumped it's not going to take a huge amount of intense deduction to work out why. There are only so many situations that can occur in a break-up scenario. But my analyzing skills plus the immense amount of pot fogging her brain put me up there with some sort of all-knowing mystic; I should have bought thumb cymbals and a zitar. This lasted for around two months. If I wasn't also so stoned at the time I would have realized I could have started charging her money for this.

Next, moving in with my brother who had just moved to London after he had left his wife of 10 years was probably a worse idea than moving in with the Indian stoner. This meant we could be depression enablers to each other and as I said, London is a great city to be depressed in. Being depressed in London is easy, being depressed in any big city is easy. Everyone either looks miserable or sad anyway, so one more long face isn't going to make much of a difference.

If you do want to be depressed in London don't drink. The depression is enough; seriously, a drinking crutch is simply enabling the depression. If you do drink and you are even mildly depressed you will find yourself in situations that aren't classed as normal weekend activities.

You will end up at strange parties, drawn in by the music. You may end up at a wedding reception uninvited but for some reason welcomed as it's, "good luck to have a stranger at a wedding," drunk or otherwise. You may end up at all night raves in abandoned warehouses or wake up in strange towns with no memory of how you got there.

You may end up sitting talking to a prostitute as she smokes crack using a coke can as a pipe after you have just given her the money to buy the crack because you felt sorry for her for turning down her sexual services not knowing she was about to use the money to buy crack and not food and thus contribute to her downward spiral.

You may end up at wandering into what seems to be another great party judging from the music but actually turns out to be a Salvation Army gathering in a church hall and for some reason have your photograph taken standing in front of the entire congregation before stealing an umbrella as you leave because it's raining out. You may invite a group of homeless people into a restaurant with you because once again you felt sorry for them only to be thrown out by the restaurant manager.

You may also wake up after a night in the police cells on intermittent occasions with no memory of how you got there, but at some point the policeman's farewell statement that you are the most paranoid person he has ever met may start to sound like an omen. You may end up in many strange, weird and sometimes risky situations with a slow nagging sensation beginning to creep in that maybe you are now unconsciously but actively looking to give yourself reasons to be depressed.

And yet, when you have left all of this and more that you cannot remember behind you, you may begin to look back on it and think – being depressed in London, it really wasn't as bad as I had thought.

The End of the Nineties

The disappearance of time is not an uncommon experience if you happen to be stoned a lot. With Sophia time disappeared a lot. Time sometimes reappeared during the working day but it was diluted, only semi real. The rough edges of the day were smoothed and soothed. Daylight appeared through a soft focus lens and everything slowed down a click.

By day we would work in separate offices in the same building, contacting each other frequently by instant message. Work was just something to be endured until five pm arrived. Then she would appear at the door of my office and motion that it was time to go and I would dutifully trot after her. As I climbed into the passenger seat of her car she would turn on the car heater and light a cigarette. In the twenty minute journey home we would talk about the day we had both had. Meaningless talk about work colleagues, people that really didn't matter to her or to me.

The warmth of the car, the familiarity of Sophia's voice and the music she would play on the car stereo would relax me and I would feel safe. Whether I knew it or not, I was, for the first time, in a very long time, happy or content. I wasn't sure which, but it felt good enough not to question.

It was winter when I lived with Sophia and it was always dark on the journey home. We would drive down dark country lanes and roads until we saw the lights of her town. Even though we lived together as housemates it was *her* town, not mine. It wasn't a town I felt safe in. I felt safer in London than here. There was an oppressive feeling about the place and I really only felt safe once we had entered the front door and locked it behind us.

Once inside and settled on the large sofas Sophia would bring out the papers, begin rolling up and time would disappear once again. Sophia would offer the joint and I would be surprised at first in my inability to refuse. After a few days my surprise disappeared and I just gave in. Every day I would tell myself that I wasn't going to smoke but every night I would do otherwise. It began to feel safe and easy, and everything about it felt good.

Our conversations always focused on our previous relationships. We had both just come out of long term relationships that had ended badly. We examined the breakup of these relationships, what went wrong and asked why they had ended the way they did. More often than not I played shrink to Sophia's patient. It was easy to do; I just put myself in her ex-boyfriend's head and gave her the answers to my breakup. Her ex sounded a lot like me. A fear of commitment compounded with an inferiority complex that he wasn't good enough for her. Sophia thought that I was psychic at times in the answers that I gave. But there was no magic involved. I didn't tell her what she wanted to hear, I just told her how it was for me and my ex, and then I switched couples.

Sometimes Sophia would burst into tears or sometimes she would just sit very silently, stoned, watching the television until ten pm. At ten she would take a shower and change into her nightclothes, have a final joint and then suddenly leave the room and go to bed. I would sit there alone, watching television until midnight before going upstairs, past her room. The door would always be shut and I would never question that.

And that was how it went, every night and every weekend. The surroundings never changed, but our relationship did. I realized that I was starting to depend on her. If she went out with friends I would miss our talks and I would wish that she was home. I tried not to think of her in any way except platonic but it didn't quite work. I wanted to be with her and yet I didn't. She was still grieving for her ex and I was still too closed off to let anyone in. If there were any signs that she wanted the relationship to be anything other than what it was, I ignored them. When time is disappearing at such a fast rate it's easy to ignore important things and just focus on the day to day, the trivial, the meaningless and safe. That way nothing gets to you. That way, you don't get hurt.

Sophia was into Tarot cards. From time to time she would spread the cards out and make me pick. I didn't really believe in it but she did, so I was happy to go along with it.

One night, semi-stoned, I asked her to read my cards. She said yes and then said, "But I'm not doing it down here, I need somewhere flat. We'll use my bed."

"We'll use my bed."

The words sounded like a whisper in my head, soft enough so that I couldn't be sure if I had heard them correctly. It doesn't mean anything, so we're using her bed, it's no big deal. There's a perfectly good floor down here where we are sitting, she just wants to be comfortable, to use her bed, in her room, where she has never invited me before. She just wants to be comfortable. Her black thong drying on the radiator in the bathroom suddenly appeared in my head. My stoned mind raced while the rest of my body was slowly turning to syrup.

"I'll go and set them up and then you come up in a few minutes okay?"

"Yeah, yeah, okay, no problem."

Except there was a problem, this would change everything. If something happened in Sophia's bedroom this would change everything. It could be great, it could be the start of something but it could be a disaster. I was an emotional cripple, I knew this. I was unable anymore to face anything that felt like real intimacy. I ignored any signal from any woman that felt as if it could mean something.

If anything happened it could be either a one night thing or it could be a start. How was I meant to know what it meant? And I will get the signals wrong, I know I will.

A couple of years ago this would not have been a problem. A couple of years ago if it was a one night stand then that would be great, if it seemed that something more was wanted then I would pretend afterwards that I didn't know what she was talking about.

That would have been me a couple of years before my last serious relationship went south and everything changed but now, now. I really liked Sophia and yet I couldn't take going through the meltdown that had occurred in my last relationship, I couldn't deal with that again. I took another drag on the joint and listened to her bumping around upstairs, and then silence.

Sophia's head popped around the door, "Come on I'm ready."

But I'm not ready. I'm not ready for this.

What happened to just sitting on the sofa talking, no pressure, just friends remember? I followed her up the stairs and into her bedroom. It was so nice compared to mine, it had that woman thing going on. Fluffy and candley and everything smelt great and she had curtains whereas my room didn't even have a lightbulb. The candles were lit and the cards were laid out on her bed.

"Come on, sit down on the bed and let's start."

She didn't go so far as patting the spot she wanted me to sit down on so I sat on the corner of the bed, almost sliding off. I started picking cards and Sophia turned them over and started talking about…something, I don't know, I wasn't listening. I just sat there smiling, talking gibberish. Yes, yes, oh you're making that up, really, yeah that really relates to me. Except now in my stoned state, everything related to me and to her and to this moment. For once, time was passing really slowly.

My heart was pounding, my stomach was tight and my paranoia was in full flow. It wasn't a trickle, it was a torrent. It was flooding the banks and drowning innocent bystanders. What do I do? I kept sneaking glances at her while not listening intently.

"This card could mean that you will be with someone that you have been through a lot with."

What the hell does that mean?
Does she mean her? Us? We've both been through a lot together, I think. I mean we're living together, we work together, we've both recently had long term relationships that ended badly and we kind of clung to each other and felt safe together at the side of the road after the car crashes.

Didn't we?

It could mean anything, there's no signs here, you are stoned, you are paranoid, everything she is saying is relating to you because you've been stoned since you moved in here with her a month ago. You make a move on her and tomorrow you're going to be the laughing stock of the work. There are going to be yellow post-it notes sticking to your back for weeks. Muted laughing by the water cooler as you walk by, whispering from the girls in her office. There are no signals. Then why are you in her bedroom with candles flickering in the darkness, sitting on her bed as she tells you your future?

"Are you okay? I'm finished." She says.
"Yeah, that was great. I, y'know, hope it comes true."

I look straight into Sophia's eyes and get off the bed. Sophia sits there staring back, saying nothing as I head towards the door.

"Okay, well thanks," I say. "I'll see you downstairs."
THERE ARE NO SIGNALS.
I start to walk away and then I look back. She's still sitting on the bed but she gives me a look, this look of, what are you doing, where are you going, and then she looks down and begins clearing the cards.

I walk slowly down the stairs in the darkness. You missed it, you had the chance and you didn't take it. Forget about tonight, there are plenty of tomorrows, you did the right thing, you stayed safe and no one got hurt. Sophia came down and sat on the opposite sofa and gave me another look. I recognized that look - disdain or scorn. Whatever look that was, it was not complimentary. But as she rolled another joint she didn't say a word.

She went to bed at 10pm and I followed her up the same stairs at midnight. Her door was shut.

A few weeks later I left Sophia's house and moved back to London. On my final day at work Sophia bought me a drink to say goodbye. Even though it was lunchtime she seemed slightly drunk. She handed the drink to me without saying a

word and then left the pub. Her only email to me that afternoon before I left for London consisted of one word.
Coward.

When you're not stoned, the disappearance of time is not uncommon. But now, time now has a way of making you see things more clearly.

Filter Image

It was 1pm and Joe was just waking up. The curtains were drawn but light was seeping, uninvited into the small living room. His first thoughts were that he hated waking up. Dreaming was a lot more fun lately than real life. Joe didn't have work to go to and he had nothing planned for the rest of the day but he knew he should be out there, looking for a job. But it was taking all of what was left of his energy just to get out of bed or should that be off of the sofa.

Joe hadn't slept in a bed now for almost a year, maybe more, since he had moved into the one bedroom flat in London with his brother. Both brothers were now living the supposed bachelor good life in fun filled London, well at least that's what the family and friends back home thought.

"You must be having a great time down there, no ties, making money, having fun every weekend, wish it was me."

This is what most of Joe's friends said to him when he phoned them at weekends, usually late at night, after a drinking session, alone in the flat, bored shitless, drinking from the bottle, waiting on unconsciousness to hit.

He then remembered whilst flipping channels that today was a bank holiday and he had to go into the centre of London, the West End, to meet Claira. His brother was working again, making money, working non-stop seven days a week. This, thought Joe, must be his way of coping. His way of dealing with his wife leaving him after 11 years of marriage, taking his child and telling him with little feeling, "You come in here every night, sit down and watch TV. Is that your idea of a marriage?"

Joe remembered this line because he had been listening in the kitchen of the house when she had said it but he couldn't remember feeling any sadness for his brother because how may marriages had he seen break up? Wasn't it just a question of time before this happened to everyone who got married? Wasn't it just taken for-granted that marriage in modern society doesn't mean life anymore? When a murderer gets a life sentence it doesn't mean life, it's just a saying, it means 15 years and usually with time off for good behaviour.

Till death us do part doesn't mean that literally, it's just something the priest says, its part of the circus, part of the act, you're not supposed to take it seriously. As if a man standing there with a dog collar on can seal the two of you together for life.

Anyway that was his brother's problem not his and his way of dealing with the issue was to work, ten hours a day, seven days a week, trapped in his own work induced prison with no parole in sight.

Joe on the other hand had taken a different route.

"So are we going to sit here all day or what?"
Claira had an annoying way of breaking into Joe's thoughts, especially when he was thinking of nothing in particular. The sun was blinding here, sitting on the steps beside Trafalgar Square, people watching. Bank holidays always brought the crowds out, milling around aimlessly, staring at each other, feeding pigeons, jumping in and out of fountains. Their skinny, white, hairy British legs clad in shorts, hopelessly trying to take a tan and noisy, shit it was so noisy compared to Joe's flat, which was peaceful and where the only decision he had to make was when to make a drink or change the channel on TV.

Now Claira was forcing him into another decision,
"What do you wanna' do?" she demanded.
Joe had seen the guy coming towards him out of the corner of his eye. It happened at precisely the same moment as

Claira had taken out her camera and was snapping away at the side of his face. He was pretending not to notice her taking pictures so he wasn't moving. This way she would only get one side of his face. She knew he hated getting his photograph taken but it seemed his opinion didn't amount to shit on something as trivial as this but now it was about to hit him from both sides.

"Hi, I'm doing a student project, I'm asking people to tell me exactly what they are thinking about at this precise moment. Do you mind telling me what you're thinking?"

"No I don't mind."

But Joe did mind. What he was thinking, shit, he was thinking…

"No lying, it has to be exactly what you are thinking right now."

Yeah I'm thinking why don't you fuck off and bother someone else. I'm thinking I am completely broke because my shit job that I walked out of last week wouldn't pay me the month's money they owe me and I have about £8 in my pocket and Claira wants to go to the pub and this is all the money I have left in the world and I don't even want to be here but because she has flown all the way over from America it would've been impolite to tell her to fuck off and leave me alone to lie on my sofa and watch bank holiday TV.

"I'm thinking I wish Claira would stop taking my photograph because she knows I hate getting my photograph taken."

"Oh, well part of my project is to take photographs of everyone I have asked this question to."

Of course Joe already knew this because he had seen the student taking the last person's photograph.

"Do you mind me taking your photograph?"

"I guess not."

The student stepped back and aimed the camera at Joe. Joe plastered on a fake smile which didn't move any part of his face except his mouth and held it.

"Thanks man." And with that the student moved on to bother his next victim with his meaningless, banal project.

"Well do we go to the pub? I've arranged to meet some friends there?"

Friends, thought Joe. More people that I don't know, that I don't want to meet, that I don't want to have conversations with about what job I'm not doing, how we met, what my life's ambitions are and really, I just don't have enough money. Four months ago Joe was making £500 a week, working two jobs but slowly he had given up both jobs, one after the other without even noticing it, and now he was unemployed but he didn't really care about this, I mean everyone knows a job isn't for life anymore is it?

Meaningless jobs in London are two a penny, he would pick one up easily enough when he needed to. Eight pounds, the figure loomed up in Joe's mind for a second. Not much but he didn't need much of anything right at this moment.

"No I'm going to go now, I have to do something."

"But you only just got here." Claira looked dejected, sad. A sadness that Joe thought made her eyes look very dead, as if there was really nothing inside.

"Why lie?" thought Joe.

"I really just don't want to meet anyone. I thought it would just be the two of us but now you bring loads of your friends into the equation and I can't be bothered making small talk and I really don't have the money to go drinking and look, I'll phone you tomorrow, I get paid tomorrow, I'll meet you tomorrow and we'll have celebration for your last day here."

With that sentence Joe stood up, lit a cigarette and walked away. The last part of the sentence was a lie. He wasn't going to get paid tomorrow and he had no intention of coming into London to meet her tomorrow. He had started off well but fell at the last hurdle to spare her feelings.

"Anyway there are plenty of tomorrows." Thought Joe as he slowly disappeared out of the sun into the darkness of the crowd filled tunnel, heading for the underground train.

Tomorrow, Claira will phone Joe constantly during the day to see when he is coming into London but lately Joe didn't answer his phone at all. He would check the display to see who was ringing although he didn't know why he did this because he never answered.

He was slowly cutting himself off from everyone he knew. His family, his friends, his relatively new, soon to be ex-girlfriend. He rarely even talked to his brother now.

He lay on the sofa and watched television and listened as the phone rang. People on the other end of the line taking time out from their lives to talk with Joe, unknowingly trying to resuscitate him from his self-induced coma. He was quietly slipping out of society and he didn't know or care why.

The Last Busker in London

Christmas Eve, the West End of London. It's an eerie feeling to be wandering around Leicester Square when it's completely deserted. I had never seen it like this before. No "hustle and bustle" on this, the supposedly busiest shopping day of the year in Britain's answer to Disneyland. Three-o-clock and already the streets are empty, save for a few lone last minute shoppers, rushing home, their arms laden with brightly coloured packages, wrapped up warm against the biting London wind. The small, merry go-round which was part of the Christmas carnival in the square is being covered up with tarpaulin, protected against the drifts of snow blowing around the streets.

The charity collecting Santas had all retired to the pubs to get drunk from their day's takings before going home and forcing their wives into an abysmal Christmas Eve legover. The vain hope lingering that maybe they could sleep through the torture of a whole day with the family and in laws that tomorrow will bring. Tiny Tim has shut up shop and gone to score some festive cheer to make it through the hohoho holiday season. No cold turkey for him. Tis the season to be wasted.

I walk on towards Piccadilly Circus, no real idea of where to go, just get out of this cold.

How I came to be cold and alone on this particular day of the year does not merit going into in great detail at this point, suffice to say that in the previous thirty years leading up to today I had been dogged by a catalogue of unrelenting failures and disasters in both my personal and professional life. A cacophony of girls had passed through my fingers, each one treated more carelessly than the last. Any money I had acquired had been gambled or pissed away and the self imposed exile that I now found myself in was a fitting karmic payoff to the debt of wrongs I had unwittingly inflicted on others.

The final straw had come with the breakdown of my last long-term but unavoidably doomed relationship with a girl nine years younger than myself. I should have seen it coming, a pattern had already been set in stone with my relationships. A three year use by date barcoded on each one. A year of fun and non stop sex and thinking that I had fallen in love, followed by a year of increasing boredom, unfaithfulness and suspicion, and finally an unbearably long year of recriminations and silences as we waded through mud towards the inevitable break up.

When I had kissed her goodbye and boarded the plane for a week in Greece with friends, I knew that when I returned my girlfriend would be gone but I didn't realise how hard this one would hit me or the severity of the meltdown that would follow. This was my third and final shot at London. This time, I had to make it count.

I swung open the door of The St James Tavern, a corner pub just off Piccadilly. It was empty, or near enough empty for me to feel conspicuous.

"Pretty dire today." I say to the lone barman.

"Yep, only the dregs left now."

"Cheers mate." Wait, did he just include me in the dregs?

I take my pint of Guinness and a Jack Daniels and take a seat next to one of the huge windows where I can look out at the other ghosts haunting the streets. A girl of about 20 passes by, blonde, very thin, very pale, heavy black shadows etched underneath her eyes. She is wearing a long shabby winter coat that looks about two sizes too big for her and keeps rubbing her arms through the heavy material. Ten minutes later she walks by again, this time headed towards Soho, her face pained, still rubbing her arms. She had better find something quick or that pain is going to get a lot worse. She stops and stares straight at me through the window as she passes by, and there it is, for a moment we have a connection, we have silently whispered hello, acknowledged each other's existence. I've made up a history for her on the basis of a first impression, my own version of what her life consisted of and more than likely vice versa. I hope she's put her imagination to good use and made it more colourful than the reality.

I know I shouldn't really be drinking because of the depressant aspects that follow the main reason to get drunk in the first place, to feel happy, and even if it's a false happiness I like the quick hit of optimism that comes with a shot or two of Jack and coke. I am thirty, I have no ties, no responsibilities, no commitments, no debts, and how many people can say that? I'm in the West End of London with plenty of cash in my pocket. I've a got a job and a roof over my head and a multitude of possibilities lay ahead.

Sure I'm alone but I don't feel lonely. Some people regard loneliness as a disease and to be honest, this is the first time in years I have been totally alone. No girl around to put my hand under her chin in the dead of night or feel her warm breath against my cheek in the morning when I awake but this is just a temporary loneliness, a mild winter cold. The disease only becomes terminal when you don't realise you're alone, when you've become used to the silence and look forward to it when you get home at night. When you've forgotten what its like to be loved and in love and when you've given up on trying, that's when you're in trouble. Shit stop feeling so sorry for yourself.

Always try and have the maximum fun with the minimum effort, live by that and time should pass quickly - in theory. I down the double Jack and coke and head back to the bar.

10.30pm. Kings Cross, O'Neils bar and I am feeling no pain. I'm even enjoying Slade blasting out Merry Christmas into my ears for what feels like the hundredth time today.

"What...so what the hell are you doing on your own on Christmas Eve Cal?"
"Well what are you two doing here on Christmas Eve?"

I'm sitting with two guys, both twenty-something recruitment consultants who have been drinking since lunchtime and had already burned their ties in the ashtray as sign that the year was over and that new ties would probably be arriving from Santa on Christmas day. No one needs more than one tie. They had invited me to join them after seeing me sitting alone at the bar.

Whereas strangers will normally avoid each other in London bars, the danger being that you could turn out to be a complete psycho after a few drinks, Christmas sometimes brings out the best in people, spirit of friendship and all that sort of stuff which usually only exists in a town called Bedford Falls in a film called It's a Wonderful Life and has more to do with the alcohol previously consumed than the time of year. We are well on our way to drinking the bar dry. I look at my reflection in the wall mirror. I wouldn't like to have your hangover tomorrow.

"I can't go home because I haven't bought my girlfriend a present. She is going to be so pissed at me, it's this fuckers fault."

"S'not my fault, I said we would just pop in here for one drink, you're the one that's been buying the doubles."

"I can't, I just can't go home with nothing. D'you think she'd appreciate a four pack of lager?"

"More drink, more drink, same again yeah?"

Mick trots off to the bar blasting out the drinks he wants on the way.

"So why you here again?" he asks me.

"Well my flatmate went home to Austria for Christmas," I slur, " and I couldn't face another Christmas back home, now I come to think of it, I've not been home for Christmas in about five years."

"Oh thas bad, thas bad, you got to be with your family at Christmas, you just gotta' be. Mick, Mick tell 'im, dont'ya have to be with your family at Christmas?"

" Shutuuup Brycey you maudlin bastard." Mick shouts planting another tray of pints and whiskey doubles on the table, "Christmas is just a big commercial rip-off designed by the advertising people to play on our guilt that because we treat our family like shit for the rest of the year we feel pressurised into buying the most expensive bottles of perfume or boxes of cigars so that the guilt will ease and we can feel better and forget about them until birthdays or mother's day come around again."

"So cynical for one so young," said Bryce clapping Mick's face, "but what about the kids, Christmas is for the kids, the little bastards, you got any kids Cal."

"I don't think so and that's another reason for not going home, the three thousand questions I'll get from my mother. When you going to settle down? When you going to get married? My brother and sister are both divorced, she seems to hold me up as the last hope."

"But still, you're going to be on your own on Christmas day man, thas not good, you cant..be..on..ah fuck it ..more drink."

"The bar's closed Bryce, no more drink, time to go home and face the music."

"Oh shit, I wish I was you Cal, all alone, no presents to buy, no worries."

"Well thanks for cheering me up mate, next time I think I'll just phone the Samaritans. Wait the bar's shut, what time is it?"

"Nearly 12."

"Twelve, shit I've gotta' get the tube, they shut early tonight don't they?"

I jump up and feel my legs starting to buckle, I've drank a lot more Christmas spirit and coke than I thought.

"Woh there, steady boy, thas it, thas it, you're fine the undergrounds jus' across the road."

I say my goodbyes and try to walk out the door in a straight line, it's difficult but I manage it. Over the road and outside the station. This is bad the doors are locked and the sign reads, 'No more trains until the 27th December, Merry Christmas.' I look around, no night buses to be seen and I've more chance getting a ride on Santa's sleigh than finding a taxi tonight. I stand for a minute and watch the last busker in London playing Silent Night on his saxophone. With the silence that surrounds me and the alcohol coursing through me, the notes that are floating into my ears have never sounded so beautiful.

I throw a ten pound note into his case just to reinforce that I am really drunk and walk on, knowing that it was a hotel or the street tonight. There is no way I can walk all the way to Wandsworth in this condition, even if I wanted to, my head will hit the pavement after an hour of pounding these streets.

I've been walking along the Caledonian Road now for about fifteen minutes and haven't spotted any vacancy signs in the bed and breakfasts or small hotels that litter the area. It's started to snow lightly and the optimism I had felt hours ago has now disappeared completely. This place is scary. Every now and then a car drives past and honks its horn. Keep walking, just keep walking. This isn't how I should be spending Christmas Eve, wait, its now officially Christmas day, I should be tucked up in bed awaiting a day with loved ones, friends and family, Christmas dinner and the same old television repeats. A bit of cold and darkness and suddenly I'm getting nostalgic for a day I don't even like that much.

"Where are you off to mate?"
I jump out of my thoughts, where had these three come from? Two guys and a girl appear at my side

"Shit you scared me, just trying to find a hotel, kissed my last train home an hour ago."

"You'll not find anything around here, everything's shut up for the night."
The guy had an accent I could almost place and although my instincts were telling me that this should make no difference, to be wary, the familiar sound of home and the amount of drink I had consumed was fogging my brain and telling me that these people were okay.

"What you been doing?" said the girl. She was quite pretty but in a rough, street sort of way, her age could've been anything from twenty to thirty-five.

"Just been out drinking with mates, Christmas you know?"

"You got any weed on you?" Said the other, dreadlocked guy.

"No, no, I've got some money though if you know where to score any."

I know I shouldn't have said this but they seemed friendly enough.

"Man, how much you got, I can get some then we'll go back to my place, it's just round the corner, you can't be wandering around here at this time of night, its not safe ya'know."

I fish into my pocket, bring out a twenty and hand it over.

"Aright you three go onto the flat. I'll meet you there in about 10."

With that he was gone and I had a sneaking suspicion so was my twenty. This must have been registering on my face as I stood there watching him walk away.

"It's alright man, he's okay, we share a flat together, c'mon its too cold to be standing about here. Where you from?"

I tell him and a look of surprise comes over his face.

"Been there many a time back in the day, stop looking so worried man, it's alright, we're just trying to help you out, Christmas and all that."

"Yeah, yeah you're right, just a bit drunk, paranoia working overtime."

We continue walking for about ten minutes making small talk until we reach an estate, blocks of flats that look less than salubrious. Rubbish litters the streets, graffiti covers the walls and the place is completely deserted.

Finally after three or four flights of unlit stairwells we enter the flat. Shit what a dump. This was a bad idea, a very bad idea.

The small living room consists of two battered old sofas, a bed pushed against the wall and a one bar electric heater. The place is filthy. Damp has made the paper peel from the walls, open tins sit around the floor with forks sticking out of them. Ashtrays heaped to overflowing with cigarette butts and finished joints are scattered around the room. Luckily for me the alcohol I have consumed has robbed me of my sense of smell. A complete dive although a London estate agent could probably make it sound desirable and flog it for well over the 150 grand mark.

I suddenly spot the works on the table. I knew it, junkies. I should have realised straight away from the shabby clothing and pasty skin. I've got nothing against drugs or junkies, I just don't want to be in this situation while still drunk and with over three hundred pounds in my pocket. So why when my mind is screaming at me not to be such a dick and to just get out of there did I say yes when the next offer came?

"You want a whisky Cal, keep out the cold?"
I take the half bottle of Bells, take a slug and feel the warmth enter my veins and swirl around the back of my eyeballs as I swallow.

"Good stuff eh?"
Before I can answer rasta walks into the room,
"Aright got the stuff no probs, you alright man?"
"Yeah, yeah fine just downing some whiskey."
"Good for you but this stuff is better."
He takes out a wrap of weed and starts to roll a joint. Ten minutes later and I'm completely wasted, my brain is mush. I try to move from the seat but my legs have become 100% putty.

"This is strong stuff." I can hear myself saying.
"Yeah it's not bad," said rasta, "but here try some of this."
He produces a white china ornament, like a teapot only smaller and holds it out to me after he has sucked on the spout, inhaling deeply whatever was inside.

"This is the real stuff try it."
"What is it?" I'm try to focus on his hand as he waves it a few feet in front of me.

"It'll make you feel good, come on Cal, have some faith, you're among friends."

I don't know what's in that jug but I am not wasted enough to try it because if I do there is no doubt in my mind that I will pass out and this is just too dodgy a situation to be unconscious in. The girl, whose name I don't know, is now in front me. My pot-fogged brain has made her now look very tempting as she begins to rub my thighs with her hands.

"Come on Cal just try it, you'll feel great."

Her voice is low and soothing, as if her throat is coated with warm honey and I could drift off to sleep just listening to her. I desperately want to sleep now, my eyes are starting to close. I see her suck on a joint and then bring her face close to mine.

"Just try it Cal."

"I just want to drift, I want to.."

I feel her lips on mine, she blows smoke into my mouth, everything is slowing down. I sink into the sofa as she rubs my thighs harder, it feels good, I'm getting hard. Wait, isn't she the other guy's girlfriend. Shit. I push her off me,

"I have go to the toilet, where is it, the toilet?"

"It's first on the right man. You alright?"

"Yeah, yeah, just need the toilet, I'll be fine."

I stagger into the small toilet and bend over the sink. My veins feel as if they've have been stuffed with cotton wool, my face is burning, I look at myself in the mirror, sort yourself out Cal, just get the fuck out of here. Throwing water over my face I suddenly remember the three hundred pounds, I thrust my hand into my pocket and bring out the roll,

"Cal, Cal you alright in there?" Rasta is pounding at the door.

"Yeah, yeah, just washing my face." I croak, taking my boot off and laying the money flat inside.

Suddenly the door bursts open and he comes rushing in shouting, "What's goin' on man, y'all right?"

"Yeah I'm fine, just feelin' a little shaky."

He stares at me as I sit on the side of the bath easing my foot back into the boot. He has to have seen it. He stands there looking around, sniffing the air. Does he think I am holding out on him, smoking weed in the bathroom on my own? Paranoia Cal, calm down.

"Aright shaky, come on I've just rolled another." he says walking out of the room.

"Great, be right through."

Screw this, I'm out of here. I push open the front door and stand on the outside landing. I'm about three floors up and the place is pitch black. I wouldn't have a clue where to go, it's a rabbit's warren. Doesn't matter, just get out of here.

"What you doing man?"

Rasta again, fuck, he's crept up on me without a sound.

"Just getting some air, that's strong stuff. Look is there somewhere I can get cigarettes round here, I'm out."

I try to sound calm but we are both eyeing each other suspiciously.

"Yah, no probs there's a garage just round the corner, hold on a minute."

He appears a few minutes later with the other guy.

"Need some fags Cal?"

"Yeah and I want to get some food."

"C'mon then the garage is about ten minutes walk, can't be walking round here on your own. I told ya, it's not safe."

As we begin walking back up the road the notion to do a runner crosses my mind but I am definitely still on the wrong side of wasted. If a taxi comes past I can just flag it down and jump in, something is not right here. It may be my paranoid imagination but I have a strong, dark, apprehensive feeling gnawing into the pit of my stomach. We keep walking, none of us saying a word, I can see the garage up ahead.

"Get some crisps. I'm starving."
"Yeah no problem."
I swing open the door to the garage shop, the fluorescent lights making me blink. The guy behind the counter stares at me as I grab a few bags of crisps and arrive at the counter. He probably had me pegged as a stoner as soon as I walked in.
"20..no 40 Marlboro."
Looking out of the shop window I can see the two of them under a street light, huddled together, smoking, talking, stamping their feet.
"Can I phone for a taxi from here?"
"No phone, there's a public one down the road but it's usually bust, £16.95."
I take out a twenty and slide it onto the counter, then walk out of the door.

"Aright Cal." Says Rasta
"Yeah, yeah got the stuff."
I start walking, the two of them are walking behind me and that's when I hear it.
"Now."
Rasta punches the side of my head and I hit the ground. I try to get up but I'm just not quick enough, another punch to the head and I'm on my back. The two of them are on top of me now. I throw a punch and one of them who slam's me back to the

ground. I don't feel scared just angry and because of the drugs my legs and arms aren't working as fast as they should. Rasta throws another punch at the side of my face.

"Stay down and you won't get hurt, stay down."

How could I have fallen for this, all the warning signs were there from the start. Had I never watched bloody Crimewatch.

"Get his boots," shouts Rasta, "the moneys in his boots."

He is frantically trying to grab my boots as I kick and twist my legs in every direction.

"Just give us the money Cal, we just want the fucking money."

He says this through clenched teeth, his mouth pressed so close to my ear I can feel his breath, his spit landing on my cheek.

"Think you can smoke our drugs and kiss our woman and get away with it."

"You fuck." I shout and using what strength I've got kick out my foot straight into his face, hitting him square in the nose. I can hear a crack as it connects. He reels back taking my boot with him, money flying everywhere. They both started scrambling for the notes. I look up and see the garage behind me, the garage attendant staring out of the window, watching us. As I push myself up a car pulls up in front of us, the police. Quickly the two of them start walking along the road as though nothing has happened, I can see one of them counting the money. The cop rolls down his window.

"What's going on here?"

I move towards them, stumbling, out of breath, "Those two mugged me, they've taken my money."

The officer of the law looks me up and down from the comfort of his car, rolls his window back up and drives away, in the opposite direction from my muggers. I wait on the car turning round but they don't, they just kept on driving. I wasn't important enough for them to merit getting out of their nice warm car on Christmas morning.

I stand staring after them in disbelief, then I turn and look in the direction of my attackers but they're nowhere to be seen. They are going to have a good Christmas now, courtesy of yours truly. There's nothing else for it. I start walking with leaden legs in what I hope is the direction of Kings Cross station.

Ducks, I can here ducks squawking, or is quacking? I open my eyes and focus, car horns blaring at me from the cabs going past. I sit up on the bench. My head is frozen, my jaw is numb and when I feel with my tongue, half my tooth, which had been a cap is missing. A girl wanders past the bench and then sits down next to me. She keeps staring at me until I look at her.

"Feels worse than it looks." I mumble.

"You want sex?" She asks quickly in a foreign accent.

I stare at her in disbelief.

"You know what I am saying, sex, blowjob £10."

I pull out a cigarette and light it.

"It's Christmas day, a holiday, shouldn't it be free today?"

"No £10 blowjob, you understand?"

"Look at me, my clothes are ripped, my face is battered. Do you think the first thing I thought when I woke up on this bench was, well now I'm in the mood to get my cock sucked by a total stranger.'

"Weirdo." she gets up and walks away.

I feel like I'm going to throw up but manage to suppress it and throw the cigarette away. Searching my pockets I find a couple of twenty pound notes and jump into one of the waiting taxis.

"Good night was it son?"

Everyone's a comedian.

"Just take me to Wandsworth."

I slump into the back of the black cab, my whole head now throbbing and look out towards a huge advertising billboard we are approaching. Two of London's finest examples of the metropolitan police, male and female, are flanking a huge jolly Santa, all three of them smiling down, their eyes following me as we drive by.

I read the words that are coming out of Santa's fluffy, bearded mouth into a balloon, "Keep vigilant, keep safe, and have a merry Christmas in the Capital."

London – Saturday Night, Sunday Morning

Why am I in King's Cross again?

The taxi driver had said something about not going south of the river but there are no trains at this time of the night from here. Maybe a late night pub will be open. And then I see it. A line of people by the side of what looks like a warehouse. I join the small queue of people being let in to the building two at a time. There is no sign outside of the entrance to say if this is a nightclub and when I get to the door the man simply asks for five pounds entrance fee. Entrance to what?

"Can I get a drink in here?"

"Drinks just inside the door."

The entrance corridor is pitch black and I practically bump up against another man standing with crates of tins containing alcohol of some sort. He also has a stand with bottles of spirits with measures hooked to the top of it.

"What do you want mate?" Says a voice with a face hidden in darkness.

"Just a can of lager."

"Nope, no lager, got cans of cider."

I buy two cans and he tells me to proceed up the pitch black stairway. This is obviously an abandoned warehouse, there are no carpets on the wooden stairs, no wallpaper or paint on the exposed brick walls and there is absolutely no lighting whatsoever.

"What you waiting on man? Get going. People is waiting here."

I proceed slowly up the stairs in the darkness, trying to adjust my eyes to see something, anything, my arms out in front of me, guiding myself by the wall. After climbing the first flight in complete darkness and now moving onto the second flight I begin to make out figures on the staircase.

I can see people lining the stairs, their faces illuminated for a split second by the flame from the lighters they are flicking on and off. I glimpse their faces looking at me for no more than a second and then darkness again. This is similar to walking through the haunted houses that were always the highlight of any carnival arriving in town when I was a child. I continue climbing and climbing the flights of stairs. How high does this go and where is it leading to? As I climb higher and higher I can still see the faces, the flames of the lighters illuminating men and women for only an instant. Eventually, finally, a darkened landing appears and I grope my way to a door that once opened leads to an immense wooden warehouse floor.

Once inside I take in the view of what looks like hundreds of people filling the floor, no music, just people sitting, drinking, talking, sleeping and shooting up. A couple are having sex by one of the huge windows that line one side of this cavernous room. The woman has her hands against the sheet of glass while the guy pushes into her from behind. No one else seems to be watching this, no one cares at all, it's no big deal, the other people are just content to occupy their little spaces on the warehouse floor, oblivious to anything else going on, happy to zone out.

I sit down after finding a space and open one of the cans of cider. What the fuck am I doing here? I look around and see a woman cradling a baby in her arms and as I stare at her, wondering why anyone would bring a child here, two pairs of legs appear in my line of focus. I don't look up.

"What are you so happy about man?" Comes the male voice.

Am I smiling? I didn't realise. I don't answer and there is silence for a few seconds.

"If we ask nicely can we have one of your cans of cider?" Says the other male voice. The voices sound familiar to me, South London, Jamaican fake but given my state of mind I have no intention of answering or looking up at their faces.

"Ah come on man, he's fucked, let's go."

And with that they are gone.

I sit alone once more staring into space until the early morning light begins to creep through the huge windows, over the wooden floors, like fingers creeping over the near comatose people covering the floor, almost reaching the spot in which I am sitting. I don't want the morning light to reach me so I push myself up and through the door and once on the landing I see another flight of stairs heading upwards, and from somewhere, I hear music.

There are no people with lighters guiding my way this time as I proceed once again up the narrow dark stairs but now I'm being guided by the muffled music that becomes slightly louder the higher I climb. The stairs end abruptly at a white door and music floats through from the other side. I can either leave now and get out of here or I can continue through this door to the next level like some sort of drugged up game show contestant. I push open the door.

The room is tiny, windowless and similar to an attic flat. A man stands behind DJ decks and music pours out of the huge speakers. Torches are attached to ropes hung from the ceiling, illuminating different sections of the small room as they swing from side to side when pushed by people. There are about 10 people in the room, male and female, some topless, dancing in the middle of the wooden floor in front of the DJ. No one turns round when I enter, no one acknowledges that I am here, they simply continue to dance as I once again find a corner, sit down and swallow another tab of E, washing it down with my second can of cider. The music sounds good, it's pounding through my body, I have this feeling that I am smiling as I watch the people in front of me emitting light trails behind them as they dance and jump around the floor, illuminated by the swinging torches. The alcohol is keeping me balanced but I know I'm too high.

   Too high for what?
Isn't this an opportunity taken?
Sophia's line that I was an empty book waiting on someone writing the pages for me comes back to me. Didn't I see a door and proceed through it without thinking first? Isn't this what life is about? New experiences? Can you see this Sophia? You didn't write these pages for me, I'm here, writing pages for myself.

   The dancing people look happy, this is all they want at this moment. They decided they wanted to dance tonight and made it happen and hundreds of people came, and I came and that's the point. Maybe this is where the workers bees end up at night, dancing in warehouses around London. But I have to leave them at some point, I have to get home, I'm going to be in New York on holiday in two days. I need to leave.
Get up off the floor.
Now!

I shuffle slowly over a bridge, I don't know which bridge this is or how I wound up moving from south of the river to north. I feel as if I've been walking for hours but it must still be early judging by the absence of people. I have severe brain freeze and aching feet. All I want to do is find a cash machine but even after wandering for what feels like hours but may actually only be around thirty minutes I still can't find one and I gave my last five pounds to get into that warehouse.

At the end of the bridge I climb down the stairs towards an embankment and start to walk along by the river wall.

Four people, two couples, are walking in front of me, chatting amongst themselves as if out on an evening stroll by the Thames. They are well dressed, wrapped up in long overcoats, scarves and hats to protect themselves against the morning chill. They look middle aged and the four of them stop and throw their heads back and laugh when one of says something that I cannot make out. The four stop and stand by the wall, looking out at the view over the Thames, arms around each other's waists, drinking some sort of clear liquid from what looks like champagne glasses. They don't look or see me as I pass by behind them but I stop as my gaze is caught immediately by something I have never seen before and which takes a few seconds to comprehend what exactly I am looking at.

In front of me, stretching as far as I can see is a line, a line made up of bodies lying by a wall. I realise from the snoring and coughing and whispering that these people, in sleeping bags or under cardboard boxes, are actually sleeping here by the river, have been sleeping here all night and I stand transfixed by this sight as the two couples once again overtake me, move on in front of me, laughing and sipping intermittently from their champagne glasses, completely oblivious or intentionally ignoring the sleepers in the open air by the River Thames on this freezing November morning. And then I too move on, following slowly behind the two couples but looking down now and again at the various faces as the four in front of me continue to chatter amongst themselves on their early morning stroll.

My feet are now fucked.

I cannot go on. I'd give all my cash for a cash machine. I just want to get home to some warmth and safety and something to drink and my duvet and...

"You need a ride?"

A taxi appears in front of me, the driver looking out of the side window shouting over to me.

"Hey man you need a taxi?"

Pushing myself off the wall I have been leaning against I cautiously peer through his window.

"Look I don't have any money. I've been trying to find a cash machine."

"Don't worry about it, get in son."

Climbing into the front seat, I thank the man and we set off.

"Where do you live son? You look as though you've had a rough night?"

"Wandsworth. I've run out of cash, which is why I'm trying to find a cash machine."

"Wandsworth okay," he says, "I'll drop you off at the bus stop that takes you to Wandsworth no problems."

"Yeah but look I have no money, I can't even pay the bus fare until I get a cash machine."

"Man, I'll give you the bus money," he sighs, shaking his head, "it's okay, just get home."

"Thanks." I decide to ask, "Why are you being so nice? This seems a bit unusual."

"Shit son. I've got kids not that much younger than you. I'd hate to think of them wandering about not able to get home."

This saviour parks across from the bus stop just east of Trafalgar Square, rakes in his bag and hands me some change.

"Just get yourself home okay."

"Thanks. I really appreciate this, thanks a lot."

He waves and I watch him drive off, and the line regarding angels in the city comes to me, even in this city. Right on cue the bus to Wandsworth pulls up to the stop. I'll be home in thirty minutes. A nice warm bus ride home and then bed.

I look down at the change in my hand and realise there isn't enough money for the bus.
But it's the thought that counts right?

New York for Beginners

We approach each other cautiously at first.
There are no hugs or kisses when we eventually find each other at the airport and I feel slightly disorientated, unsure about actually being here or what is going to happen over the next 10 days.

"You look dazed."

"I just had the weirdest dream on the plane and I can't really hear right because my ears haven't popped yet. Can we get a coffee somewhere here?"

"We'll get one in the city. I don't think anything here is open. Come on, let's go."

The outside of the airport is dark and expansive, filled with anonymous looking buildings. I had expected to see New York in front of me or at least somewhere in the distance but Oz isn't about to reveal itself that easily.

"I told you to bring a winter coat." Jade says on the bus ride to the train station.

I look down at my grey woollen overcoat underneath which I am wearing only a black jumper.

"This is a winter coat."

She shakes her head, laughs and then holds onto my arm, seemingly happy that I am here and we proceed onwards, closer.

My apprehension and anxiety has all but left me now.
We're in a bar somewhere in Manhattan having drinks after dropping off my bags in Jade's apartment in Brooklyn and then grabbing something to eat in a small diner themed as a fifties restaurant. It's now an hour before midnight, which means that with the time difference it's now 5am UK time, at least I think so. It's too confusing so I decide not to follow the time

difference guidelines and just stick to U.S. time. I never wear a watch and I'm on holiday, so time really shouldn't make any difference anymore.

The night continues with a few more bars, talking to strangers who all seem friendly enough. In one bar we end up sitting with a group of people and when I try to buy a round of drinks Jade tells me that people don't do that here.

One guy tells me about being laid off from his financial job and how his only desire now is to become a chef but he has no qualifications and I drunkenly tell him just to go for his dream and use the severance money he received to fund it, and he tells Jade that I am nicest person he has met in New York. And the night continues in this vein for a while, drinks, drinks, talking non-stop, Jade wanting to play pool, more drinks kissing Jade by the pool table and then…..

I'm on a subway on my own. The train is packed with early morning commuters, some of whom are staring at me. I try and remember what happened last night and where Jade went to but I can't, it's a blank even though it was only hours ago. I look at the man sitting opposite me who looks back and I take a chance.

"Is this," I start to speak through a very dry mouth, "does this train go to Brooklyn?"

"Yeah," He nods his head, "Where you going to?"

I rake through my pocket to find the piece of paper that has Jade's address written down and tell him.

"Ah okay, yeah I'll tell you when we get there." He smiles.

You see, people in New York aren't rude. They're friendly and helpful, even at this hour.

"First night of my holiday. Think I overdid it."

"That'll happen." He gives me a conciliatory laugh.

Okay, I can get to Brooklyn then phone Jade and then I'll get some sleep. The train immediately slows down and comes to a stop, I'm guessing, before my stop. An announcement comes over that everyone must disembark and wait for the next train.

The kind stranger stands up, "Just get the next train and get off at Bedford Avenue. No problems."

Screw this, I need coffee.

"What can I get ya?"

The old man, who could have passed as a double for Albert Einstein, stands beside a gleaming gargantuan steel coffee machine in a shop already, at this early hour, filling up with customers.

"Just a black coffee."

"What?" he says with surprise, his accent straight out of the New York movies I had seen all my life, "You want foam on the top?"

"No, just a black coffee."

"Aw come on kid. I can make ya a cappuccino."

"No really, I just want a black coffee."

"I can make you the best latte in New York with this thing, they're the best."

Another old man walks over to him behind the counter.

"Give the guy his coffee. He only wants a black coffee."

"You know how much I paid for this thing and he only wants a black coffee." The black coffee at the end of his sentence was said as a question and definitely with much exasperation.

"Just give him his coffee and let him sit down for Christ sake." He barks this as though he has been through this routine a thousand times.

"Black coffee, okay. I don't know. What was the point in me shelling out all this cash for a machine and he only wants a black coffee?"

"Just give him the coffee will ya."

"Here ya go kid, one black coffee." Much of which he manages to spill into the saucer, "Enjoy."

It's 7am in the morning, I'm hung over to shit on the first morning of my holiday after being up for 29 hours straight and I feel at home in this city already.

A couple of hours later and after a phone call in which I give Jade directions to where I am and she tells me in no uncertain terms not to move from where I am, I'm back in her apartment.

"It doesn't matter how many times you ask me I have no idea where I was last night. I was probably just lost and wandering about."

"Well you're back safely and that's all that matters."

I can tell what she is thinking. She's thinking, is it going to be like this for the rest of the holiday? And yet at the same time I get the feeling she's not laying down any rules or restrictions but has more of a, 'what happens happens' outlook.

"So," she says as we lie on the bed, I just want to go sleep but I don't mind talking as long as I can close my eyes, just for a short while, "I have to work days so you are going to be pretty much left on your own to your own devices. We have the nights and the weekends free and as it's Thanksgiving this week I have a few extra days free. Are you okay with that?"

"Absolutely, no problem."

Although I want to spend time with Jade I'm also thinking that it could also be kind of exciting exploring the city on my own and then spending the nights together.

"I'm going to give you my cell phone for during the day and it has my work number in it so you can get in touch if you need to."

"Do you think I'll need to? I have been abroad on my own before."

"I think you will need to judging by last night. Plus it means *I* can keep in touch with you."

The electronic tagging device disguised as a phone.
I don't blame her.

And so for the rest of that week I wander the city on my own during the days. Every day I take the train into Manhattan and explore the famous places I have only seen in films. Times Square is a sensory overload of lights and noise, and I use it as my base; if I get lost I always head back to Times Square and can easily find my way from there, whether it's back to Brooklyn or to meet up with Jade in the city. I spend hours in coffee shops and bars and bookstores and record stores just browsing until I realise I am really just killing time until I can meet up with Jade when she finishes work.

One day I board the Staten Island Ferry and this is the day I realise how cold the weather here actually is. I take my place outside at the front of the ferry as the trip begins. Looking behind me I notice a lot of people staring through the glass and realise at the same time that I am the only person outside on the deck. Within a few minutes, as the ferry picks up speed, I begin to freeze, I can't move. My face becomes numb with the cold as the ferry moves quickly across the water. The pain to my face is intense, the cold seems to be ripping right through my skin like shards of glass but I don't want to go back inside. To the people staring at me through the glass I must seem like a typical tourist idiot, either that or some sort of below zero temperature masochist.

Jade's cell phone begins to ring in my pocket but I can't answer it. As soon as I take my hands from my pockets they freeze and I can no longer move them to answer the phone.

But at least I witness the view of New York from the river. I probably would have had a better view if my eyes weren't streaming with water. But all the same, this was a view I had waited years to witness and in front of me, as the Statue of Liberty passed and the skyscrapers stood guard on the city's life I now knew, by this view alone, why they call New York the capital of the world.

Each day the city opened up to me a little more. Not only the places I wandered through but the people, the characters who lived here, the daily street theatre, which also existed in London but which seemed to be in widescreen high definition here. People watching is one my favourite past times, observing everything, listening to the accents, looking out for the mad ones, and the mad ones, they did appear.

The man wrapped up in an enormous jacket who stood beside me while waiting for a subway and looked me up and down and shook his head and simply said, "Oh boy." The old woman with the long grey hair who got off the train and screamed straight into my face for no reason at all except that I was standing in front of the door she was coming through. The young man outside of the guitar shop who stood peering in through the window as I browsed inside and who had the darkest, most haunted eyes I had ever seen on someone so young. The four drag queens who sat at the diner counter drinking coffee and laughing amongst themselves as if this were most normal thing in the world.

Everyone I spoke to always commenting on my accent, asking where I came from, why I was here, taking an interest. I would regularly get lost for hours on my daytime wanderings but I didn't care, it was part of the adventure.

Apart from the daily phone call from Jade to arrange where to meet at the start of the evening, time really didn't matter here. I was in another world, far from London, and that city, with all its problems seemed, in only the space of few days, like a lifetime ago. There was nothing about New York that I didn't like and right here, London ceased to exist.

By night, Jade and I would meet and tour the bars, restaurants, comedy clubs and off Broadway plays. One play we went to, based on some Bukowski short stories, was performed in a theatre so tiny you could reach out and almost touch the actors while another play, which starred an Oscar winning actress performing in a Pinter production and to which we gained admittance after buying tickets on the street from a scalper, was set in an immense, majestic looking Broadway theatre.

    We would explore the bars of the East Village and Greenwich Village and Brooklyn - dive bars, jazz bars, bars where they were showing pornographic films on huge television sets. Jade would stick a credit card behind the bar and open a tab and we would then drink and talk for hours, and much to my happiness the bars, as I had heard, really did open until the very early hours, it wasn't a myth, there was no, 'finish your drinks please' at 11pm as there was in London.

    Eventually we would leave the bars in the small hours and wander the streets of Manhattan, not caring that the temperature was probably somewhere near or below zero. We missed the Thanksgiving Day Parade due to a severe hangover, mine of course, and even missed dinner that evening with some of Jade's friends but again, it didn't really matter to me. Right now I was in a city where every day was better than the last and the next day held something new and even exciting, and I didn't think once about having to leave this city, until….

"Stay."

It's almost closing time or at least people are beginning to leave the bar. The band has finished playing except for one old guy sitting playing the piano as the drunk and not so drunk begin to drift out of the door. It's late, actually it's early, actually I'm not sure what time it is, past midnight at least. Only 10 minutes ago this place was so full you were crushed against everyone else. People were dancing and shouting and it was hard to get a drink at the bar and now, now it's empty.

We are sitting at the bar next to where the band was playing, watching the old guy play some sort of slow jazz tune.

Jade doesn't look at me and I don't look at her, and I don't answer her one word request but continue to look at the old guy, who must be around 70, playing the piano.

"Stay." She repeats.

I have to answer but I don't know what to say. My plane back to London leaves tomorrow night. This is an impossibility. I cannot stay here no matter how much I want to. I try to make light of it, say something because really a request to stay demands some sort of answer.

"If you get the barman to play My Funny Valentine, which is about the only jazz song I know, then I'll stay."

Jade goes over to the old man and leans over and says something and I hear the old man reply, "I know it."

He begins playing and singing the words as Jade returns to her seat.

But this isn't a real deal, it's a drunken deal, a very drunken deal made in a bar in Manhattan during the early hours so it doesn't count, especially not now that the bar lights have come up and the old man stops playing and softly shuts the lid to the keys of the piano.

I don't know when or where I lost Jade.
I try calling her from the payphone in the bar but she doesn't answer. It's daylight outside but the bar I'm sitting in is almost empty. Two women are standing at the bar laughing, speaking to the barman and occasionally glancing over at me.

I hear the barman say loudly enough for me to hear, "You girls can do better than that."

I must look like shit because a torrential downpour had woken me from my slumber on the bench I was lying on only a few hours earlier, and after sheltering in a doorway for a while and smoking cigarettes and watching the rain I had made my way to my home point of Times Square where I had found a side street bar that apparently doesn't close.

I wander the bars around this area for hours until it gets dark. I am drunk enough not to bother about how I look or to be careful of any dangers that could come my way. But it's not like that here, everyone is friendly, everyone wants to talk, to make conversation. Even at this hour in the morning there are people sitting alone at the bar. I make conversation with one guy who has come into the city from New Jersey to meet his girlfriend and we talk about the feasibility of me simply staying in New York. This guy tells me it's easy and he could get me a job in his uncle's garage in New Jersey, and then he is gone and I just sit on my own and think about staying.

I think about staying until I ask myself why I would be staying and I have no answer. I love this city, I love it more than London that's for sure so why don't I just stay, why don't I just stay with Jade in her apartment? And my mind keeps saying 'because' because what?

At one point I buy postcards to send home but I leave them in a bar because really, I have no one to send them to.

It's dark again by the time I get back to Brooklyn. Jade is standing outside her apartment and bursts into tears when she sees me.

"I've called the cops. Where have you been?"
"I don't know, just wandering."
"You've been gone all night, all day. You've missed your plane."
"I just need to go to sleep. I can get the plane tomorrow. I just need some sleep."

We lie on the bed. It's only early evening but we lie there in the darkness and I try to sleep. I should be on the plane back to London right now. Did I do this on purpose? I know I'm going back. Maybe I just wanted one more day but I didn't spend that one more day with Jade although I could have and there's my answer.

The only truthful and honest answer to the question of why I should stay has to be Jade, but it's not.

And When the Arguing's Over…

Readers note: Many of these plays/conversations were written without consideration to the gender of the characters. This means the characters can be performed or read as either men or women. Plays such as *Happily..ever, Appraising*, *Hecklers* and *The Seawall* are written without mention of the character's gender. It is up to the reader to assume the gender of each character. *Algeciras* and *The Elephant Frowned* do give clues to the character's gender throughout but could quite easily be played by either men or women.

Arguing (verb) - In logic and philosophy, an argument is an attempt to persuade someone of something, by giving reasons or evidence for accepting a particular conclusion.

"The moment we want to believe something, we suddenly see all the arguments for it, and become blind to the arguments against it." – George Bernard Shaw

"I don't know about what happened... because once you start writing, it ALL becomes fiction." – Storytelling, Todd Solondz

*Plays have been set in double-space for easier reading

Hecklers

"Oh come on, come on! You think I deserved that?"

"You obviously don't. I'm not saying you deserved it but it is part of your job. To deal with them, with the hecklers."

"Fuck that. It was over the top, she was over the top. She was shouting at me as if I'd stuck a lit cigarette up her arse."

"You can't do that sort of material and not expect a reaction."

"Did you hear the fucking language coming from her?"

"It was ripe right enough but it wasn't just her."

"She started it, first her then her friends. I bet they were students."

"I'm not sure about that."

"Well I didn't deserve it. I'm trying my best out there. I'd like to see them pull that shit with Dave Mac, they'd be thrown out and they'd deserve it."

"Why did you use that joke? It's not even your kind of material."

"I'm trying to be edgier, you know, appeal to a younger crowd. This sort of stuff is in at the moment, least I thought it was."

"Don't follow trends."

"Oh now you're a fucking expert on comedy? Why didn't that occur to you at the rehearsal? Hindsight's a great thing isn't it?"

"I thought it was good, most of it was funny. I'm not a critic."

"Well you're the only one who isn't, judging by that crowd. Calling me chauvinistic, misogynistic, what a bitch."

"Why did you decide to stick that joke in, it just.."

"What?"

"It just doesn't fit in with the rest of your act."

"Now we hear it? This is one of the topics of this year's festival, you know that. There's always a new trend and I saw at least five other stand-ups using that same subject within their show during the opening week, at least once, even just one joke."

"But it doesn't fit in with the rest of your act. You saw these other stand-ups and thought what? You'd jump on the band wagon?"

"This is how stand-up works, how the history of it works, especially with the comedy festival. I'm going for edgy and you need to have something topical and right now *that* is fucking topical. Dave Mac uses it in his show and he's sold out for the entire festival."

"Dave Mac is a television star. He could masturbate standing on stilts for an hour and people would pay to see it, people would expect it. That doesn't mean he's any good."

"You're saying Dave Mac isn't good? He's a fucking headliner, he's the best."

"Well that's a matter of opinion. Look I'm not saying he's not good but you shouldn't just do those sorts of jokes because he's doing them. Next year he'll be doing something different, are you going to follow that as well. You have enough good material of your own."

"Some people laughed at it. It was that bitch and her friends. Those right-on left wing fucking students."

"I honestly don't know if they were students."

"They're always students."

"Maybe. Although maybe heckling is good."

"You think?"

"Yeah maybe. You know like Lenny Bruce was always getting heckled at first because his material was that original some people couldn't get to grips with it."

"Yeah, yeah, you think?"

"Except your material wasn't original. I mean you thought that joke up, it just wasn't your original idea."

"I wasn't plagiarising."

"I know but you're jumping on a trend. It's no big deal. Leave it out if you can't deal with the hecklers."

"I can deal with hecklers. The day I can't give a comeback to some fucking up herself little student is the day I give up on this."

"Okay."

"I just don't understand it. You know Tommy Righteous, he used the same topic in his show, I mean Tommy fucking Righteous. He used a string of these jokes and there was a write up about him the next day, calling him the must see stand-up, the festival discovery. He's going to be packed out every night after that review."

"I was thinking of going to check him out."

"I've got to see his act, definitely. What the fuck am I doing wrong? He gets accolades and I get a bitch throwing a jug of warm beer over me."

"Maybe you should just stop concerning yourself with what others are doing and concentrate on creating your own stuff, original stuff."

"I've got to keep up with what's going on, you have to. Themes, topics, they change every year, this is how it works."

"And who decides these themes, topics, every year?"

"Headliners like Dave Mac that's who."

"Right. But the audience know what they're getting from him? They expect it. No one can really complain because they're going in there to see him and they know what to expect."

"Dave Mac gets heckled."

"But that's part of his act. The audience love him and they love heckling him because his comebacks are superb, he feeds off the heckling and it's become part of his act."

"So?"

"They have one Dave Mac already, in fact they've got more than one. They don't need another one. There's enough comedians already jumping on his coattails."

(Barman comes over)

Barman

"Hey hey. How's it going?. You alright? Rehearsing your show?"

Comedian

"What?"

Barman

"Rehearsing your lines? If I didn't know you who you were I'd have thought you were a lunatic."

Comedian

"There's a fine line. Ah I didn't realise. Yeah, yeah, going over some ideas, new stuff."

Barman

"You want another drink?"

Comedian

"No. No, I'm going to catch Tommy Righteous's act."

Barman

"Ah I saw him Wednesday night. There's always one each year. Headed for big things that one. Fucking genius so he is."

Comedian

"Yeah. I don't know where he gets his ideas from."

Barman

"Beats me."

Comedian

"Okay I'll see you later."

Barman

"Enjoy yourself. You'll maybe get some inspiration.

Algeciras

Man

Are you always that aggressive?

Woman

You seemed to be into at the time, you didn't say anything.

Man

I'm not talking about that. I meant when we met last night. The way you talked to me, you were pretty aggressive.

Woman

Was I?

Man

I heard you speaking to your friend, the drunk one who fell over. Before you had even spoken to me you looked over and I heard you say to your friend that I was a prick.

Woman

We were all drunk. Come on don't get sensitive.

Man

I'm not, it doesn't bother me. I just can't remember anyone being that aggressive.

Woman

Well it worked, so you couldn't have been that bothered at the time.

Man

I wasn't, but you know, calling someone a prick seems a strange way to pick someone up.

Woman

I'm not like that usually, that's not me, well not usually. I don't know why I was being like that. Too much drink and I was nervous I guess, insecurities.

Man

What do you have to be insecure about?

Woman

The same as everyone else. I don't know. The clock was ticking towards closing time and I didn't want to end up alone last night.

Man

You have problems picking up guys? With your attitude? Shocker.

Woman

I don't have problems picking up guys. I have problems picking up guys that I would want to wake up with the next day.

Man

Failed yet again.

Woman

If I didn't want to be here you wouldn't have even heard me leaving. I've been awake for an hour.

Man

Doing what?

Woman

Just lying here, thinking. I did get up and check out your place though.

Man

(NO RESPONSE)

Woman

You just moved in?

Man

Two years ago. Rental. I don't see the point in really doing anything with it. I didn't actually think I'd be here this long.

Woman

Even though you don't own it you can still do something with it. Hanging some art on the wall would be a start.

Man

How's your hangover? Do you have one?

Woman

No not really. You?

Man

Slightly, not too bad. I find that silence usually helps.

Woman

(whispers to herself)

That must be why you don't have a TV then.

Man

What time is it?

Woman

About eleven I think. We could go out, get something to eat maybe.

Man

(No Response)

Woman

Just a suggestion.

Man

I don't really eat much in the morning, especially not after a night out.

Woman

Look if you want me to leave just say so.

Man

You wouldn't be offended?

Woman

I probably would be slightly offended and I'd probably spend a few hours wondering why you wanted me to leave and I'd probably come to the conclusion that you just wanted a one night thing. Then I'd think some more about it and I'd probably think that you were pretty rude and was it really such a hardship to speak to me for a while after we'd exchanged bodily fluids but then I'd come to the conclusion that you were probably just an asshole and there are plenty of them about so I would simply end up forgetting about it because life's too short.

Man

You could always just skip to the life's too short part.

Woman

It's cool, I'll just go. I've done the one night stand thing and been in your place, don't think I haven't. I thought we could spend a little time together that's all, my mistake.

Man

How many?

Woman

What?

Man

One night stands?

Woman

I'm not a guy, I don't count but I could always run home and check the notches on my headboard for you. Does it fucking matter? Are we having a double standards moment?

Man

Stupid question, forget it.

Woman

Forgotten.

Man

You don't have to go, really.

Woman

Don't do me any favours.

Man

Standing there pulling on your jeans is kind of changing my mind.

Woman

Wow, thanks, can I really stay? Maybe for another seven minutes or six at a push. Your home is so warm and comforting I really don't want to leave.

Man

Just get back into bed. Your body heat saves me switching on the heating.

Woman

So is this something you do a lot? One night stands then kick them out the door.

Man

I didn't kick you out the door, you decided to leave.

Woman

You're not exactly begging me to stay.

Man

I just, I find it easier, I..

Woman

Spit it out.

Man

I usually go to their place, it's easier to leave. I don't usually bring anyone back here.

Woman

So you do do this a lot?

Man

Not really. It's not like I'm in my twenties anymore.

Woman

Why is leaving immediately such an issue? I mean that is something you would do in your twenties after a one nighter. At our age you might consider the possibility that last night might lead onto to something more maybe.

Man

I don't consider it.

Woman

Never? You have a girlfriend? I'm pretty sure you didn't say anything about it last night. Wouldn't be the first time though.

Man

No, no girlfriend.

Woman

You just don't want anything more?

Man

Right. I'm on my own and I like it that way.

Woman

That's no way to live. I mean is that even living? You're happy with that?

Man

I'm not unhappy. You get used to it. It's easier.

Woman

Relationships can be hard work, yeah, but, you don't ever plan again to have a relationship, I mean a permanent one?

Man

I have no plans. Why does everyone have to have plans? I like my life the way it is.

Woman

That's kinda' seems a lonely way to go through life.

Man

I have plenty of people in my life, more than enough actually.

Woman

But this, right now, you don't like this? Having someone when you wake up? Having someone you contact during the day, who will be there for you? You know, love.

Man

I just don't do relationships, not anymore. I've learnt. The definition of insanity is to do the same thing over and over and expect a different result.

Woman

And there's a hundred and one other clichés out there that will help you through the day.

Man

You asked. I'm trying to explain, even though I don't have to. You're under the impression that everyone needs someone else, some significant other in their life. That's not always true.

Woman

I think someone got to you in the past.

Man

Now that is a cliché.

Woman

Okay. Okay. It's just conversation.

Man

Being alone is scary for many people, I understand that. I just don't see it that way.

Woman

Well even a dog can get used to sleeping in the rain if it does it long enough.

Man

Thank you Buddha.

Woman

Look all I was talking about was getting to know one other, hooking up from time to time even. The sex was good, why not? No strings. We're older, we're adults, it's quite easy. Plenty of people do it.

Man

But then it becomes a regular thing, it always does because sooner or later someone always wants more.

Woman

I'm suggesting no strings attached sex and you're saying no. This is a first I swear. You don't believe me that it couldn't be just that?

Man

No. I don't.

Woman

Why?

Man

You know, these conversations are what I don't like. Having to explain myself.

Woman

Excuse me. Why didn't you just go home and jerk off last night? You could have saved yourself all this grief.

Man

Jesus.

Woman

You know we are in a relationship right now, we're having a relationship. No matter how short - this, you and me, right now, it's a relationship.

Man

And it's temporary.

Woman

Okay look I get it, no problem. In all honesty though, from my point of view, I think you probably do want a relationship, just not with me, and that's fine, either that or you're scared.

Man

You're right, I'm terrified.

Woman

Deny all you want but this sort of thing is not uncommon once you hit a certain age and things have not panned out the way you planned.

Man

I told you I've never had any plans.

Woman

You've had long term relationships, I know that because you said you didn't do relationships but you followed that with not anymore and it sounds to me as if they haven't worked out and you've given up trying, and that's fear not this excuse of having your life just the way you want it that you're claiming.

Man

Remind me to cancel that therapy session I had booked, thanks.

Woman

Joke all you want, which is another well-worn deflection device people use but I know what I'm talking about.

Man

Okay, as you have completely worn out my patience here's a story for you.

Woman

I've got a feeling this one isn't going to have a happy ending.

Man

I used to visit a place in Spain called Algeciras. The first time I visited I went for a weekend, then I went for three months and then I went every year after that first visit, sometimes twice a year, more if I could. I equated Algeciras with happiness but the thing was I couldn't stand it when the time came to return home. Returning home got to be so bad that I decided to stop going there altogether. Feeling that down after being happy for a week, even a weekend, it just wasn't worth it. I've not been back there for almost…I think it's probably two years now.

Woman

That's not really a story but I get the feeling that is a well-rehearsed speech.

Man

Only in my head.

Woman

But that is exactly what I'm saying about not trying. And honestly it's kind of lame.

Man

Again, thanks.

Woman

No, but what? You're giving me this as an example of why you don't do relationships? Because you feel shit when they end? If that's the case where's the risk, where's the fun? Not every relationship has to be long term.

Man

I'm just having a break, taking some time off, there's nothing wrong with that. Jumping from one relationship to the next, it gets tiring. Someone said once that people spend more time choosing their car than their partner and I believe that.

Woman

I'm not disagreeing with you on that one but... let's see, here's a story for you.

Man

Go ahead, I've got plenty of time.

Woman

Time, exactly. My house, I love my house, I mean I really love that house. I've lived there for ten years now. It's a solid building, it's been standing for over hundred years and it's going to be standing long after you and I are gone. People have lived there before me and people are going to live there after me. Families are going to be living there and filling that house with life a hundred years after we've turned to dust and are no longer even a memory, and that makes me feel happy not sad.

Man

That's not really a story.

Woman

Then you're not really listening. I think I'll leave now.

Man

Stay for a while.

Woman

Why?

Man

We can waste some time together.

Woman

Until one of us gets fed up with the other.

Man

That's usually the way it works.

Appraising

Small office setting. Two employees talking.

Employee 1

I just don't see why I have to go through this. It's totally depressing and it won't change anything.

Employee 2

It's a requirement, office procedure, it's not going to hurt.

Employee 1

It'll hurt me. That asshole hates me, you know that.

Employee 2

Just sit there, listen to the spiel and it'll be over.

Employee 1

Spiel is right. Business jargon bullshitter. Screw that. I'm not lying, I'm telling it straight, what I think.

Employee 2

That's not a good idea and do you think everyone in this place doesn't already know what you think of this company, of the boss? Walking out halfway through last month's sales meeting to have a cigarette kind of gave it away.

Employee 1

That's why I know I'm going to get shat on during this appraisal.

Employee 2

Be like me, I keep telling you. Do your job and shut the fuck up. This is an easy gig.

Employee 1

No it's not and I don't know why you think that. We should be getting paid a lot more for the work we do. It's bullshit.

Employee 2

Then leave and find a better paid job or quit complaining.

Employee 1

It's just not that easy to go out and find a great job, you know that. And do you think I'm going to get a great reference from here, no chance.

Employee 2

So you hate being here and you're putting the blame on not leaving because of the reference you might get? The path you choose in life has nothing to do with your employer, that's your responsibility. I don't know why you make it so hard for yourself, live with it, plenty do.

Employee 1

I think I'm depressed.

Employee 2

You're not depressed, you're just pissed off, there's a big difference. Believe me, I know.

Employee 1

I feel trapped. Just seeing this building every morning makes me depressed. I feel my stomach sinking every single day, knowing I have to spend another eight hours here.

Employee 2

And yet you come in every single day, just like I do, just like everyone here does. You've been here two years already, if you really wanted to leave…. well.

Employee 1

Even hell will give you an incentive not to reach for heaven.

Another office. Employer and employee 1 sit across from each other.

Employer

You know, out of all my employees I feel you are the one I am least in simpatico with and I realise that some of that might be my fault. I don't think we've ever really talked at all except in an employer employee manner.

Employee 1

Well you are my boss.

Employer

That doesn't mean we can't have friendly conversation now and again.

Employee 1

It's just work, it's nothing personal.

Employer

Good employer employee relationships are the foundation of a harmonious workplace, wouldn't you agree?

Employee 1

I think there are also other important considerations.

Employer

Good, get me up to speed on your thoughts. I'd like to hear them. Maybe I can take them on board and implement them into the system. We are all about robust system processes.

Employee 1

(whispers)

Good grief.

Employer

Excuse me?

Employee 1

I've been here two years and never had a pay rise although I was promised that I would get one after being here six months.

Employer

Straight to the point, money.

Employee 1

You can't expect good employer employee relationships if you don't keep promises or pay workers a decent salary.

Employer

You don't think you are paid a decent salary?

Employee 1

I take a bus to work you've just bought a new Mercedes, what do you think?

Employer

I've helped built this business up in the last ten years, you've only worked here for two. But really, how you spend your salary is your business.

Employee 1

I've worked here two years and never had the promised salary increase.

Employer

I'm sure you'll find in your contract that it states the salary increase wasn't a guarantee, only that your salary would be reviewed before a decision was made on an increase.

Employee 1

So you reviewed it and decided I didn't deserve an increase?

Employer

Well you know there are a lot of variables to be considered.

Employee 1

Variables?

Employer

Yes, such as how much profit the company has made in the previous year and how your work in particular is a benefit towards increasing the company's profits.

Employee 1

And you feel my work has not been of any benefit to the company?

Employer

You told a customer last week that they wouldn't need our product, that it was unnecessary and that it really wouldn't help them in any way whatsoever. You basically told them to save their money.

Employee 1

What?

Employer

Isn't it true that this is what you told a customer during a sales call?

Employee 1

How do you know that?

Employer

Customer service satisfaction checks. Someone we hire calls the workplace to gauge employee service levels, to find out if they are giving customers the service they deserve. We do it regularly. Like a secret shopper.

Employee 1

But that's spying.

Employer

It's not spying, I regard it as staff training and this method is outlined in the staff handbook. This procedure helps me to locate a problem, if I think there is a problem, and then I can work out how to fix that problem. I pay you to do a job, part of which is to sell our products to customers. A customer phones wanting to buy one of our products and you persuade them otherwise? Would you call that a benefit to our company?

Employee 1

Would you rather I lied and told them we could help them? I consider what I did to be better customer service than lying to the customer.

Employer

It's not lying to point out how our products could be of benefit to the customer.

Employee 1

Customers aren't stupid. If that had been a real customer and I'd sold them something that would have been of absolutely no use to them then don't you think that would have given this company a bad reputation?

Employer

You know our products, you know that they can be of use to everyone. You should have pointed that out.

Employee 1

Only because our products are the type where there is no comeback for us if it's of no use to the customer. We can sell them this advice, if that's even what it even is, but it doesn't mean they need it or can use it. It's like life coaching, if it works then fine, if it doesn't then it's not our fault but some people simply don't need it and to tell them they do is a lie.

Employer

So you don't value our product, is that what you are trying to tell me?

Employee 1

I value it in the same way as I value a horoscope. It's pretty much on that level. People can read whatever they want into it.

Employer

Whether you value it or not doesn't really make any difference to me. Whether you do your job, which is to sell it, does make a difference.

Employee 1

So you're basically telling me to lie to the customers?

Employer

It's not lying if you point out the benefits instead focussing on how the product would be of no use. Everyone can benefit from it at some point or other.

Employee 1

Omitting the negatives is as bad as lying if you ask me.

Employer

That's maybe the way you do things but it's not the way we do things. This is work, it's not ethics one on one. We're here to make money, to be profitable. If we're not profitable then who do you think has to answer to the owners?

Employee 1

You?

Employer

That's right.

Employee 1

Well that's why you get the big bucks right? To handle the problems, to keep staff in line, to make sure your employees lie to the best of their ability.

Employer

You think you have to lie for a living? That's what I'm getting here. I'm deducing from this that you therefore think that as sales manager I am lying on a grander scale.

Employee 1

You're paid more to make sure your sales team keep lying to the customers, that's why you make the big money. You're the one who stands at the monthly sales meeting and gets the employees to believe those lies in the first place. Your bosses pay you to ignore the fact that you're telling lies to sell crap.

Employer

If that's the case then why have none of the other employees complained about the situation? Why do I only have this problem with you?

Employee 1

Believe me not everyone is as patriotic about this company as you think they are. There are many out there who know they are selling crap, they just put up with it. Fuck, half the employees here are on anti-depressants.

Employer

And just how, tell me, do I get these employees to swallow your line of thinking, that we are selling the customers a lie.

Employee 1

That's an easy one to answer.

Employer

Tell me, I'd like to know. I've been doing this job for nearly a decade and I'd like to know how you think I've been getting employees to completely buy into my lies.

Employee 1

That's simple, two words – business jargon.

Employer

Business jargon?

Employee 1

Absolutely. You make it sound, using business jargon, plausible, and for many employees that's enough. They don't understand half of what you are talking about at a sales meeting because of the nonsensical business jargon you spout but it sounds plausible and it sounds professional and for many that's all it takes.

Employer

And you are the only employee who is smart enough to see through the business jargon right? Every other employee is too stupid to see what's really going on - but not you.

Employee 1

I told you, not everyone believes it but many have too much to lose. They have families, mortgages, debts to be paid, they are scared to lose their jobs. Many have been here longer than you and would rather just swallow it and do their jobs.

Employer

Okay. You know why you haven't had a pay rise in the past, if we're being honest here?

Employee 1

I'd like to know.

Employer

Because you're a *fuck up*. You're not a benefit to this company but you're not a loss either. You're just simply here making up the numbers, doing the dog work. I should get rid of you but it would cost me more to hire and train someone else to do your job. You do the minimum amount of work with the minimum amount of effort and I pay you the minimum amount of money I can and you still put up with it. You hate this job, I know it, I can see it in your attitude but you won't make the effort to do anything else. You're one of the cogs who will sit and do their job and complain about it, but in ten year's time you'll still be here stuck in the same place you were when you first joined this company.

Employer 1

I still won't lie for you. At least I have that.

Employer

But you won't try to change anything either. You talk about the others who swallow it and do the job, you talk about them as if you're above them. But you know what, you are in exactly the same place as them, the same place that all of us are here, you're no different at all. And if I wanted to, I could make you fall into line and buy my business jargon and sell our products exactly the way I want you to.

Employee 1

How?

Employer

That's simple - two words.

Employee 1

Which are?

Employer

Pay rise.

Happily…ever…

"I'm not doing this every time we go out. I'm not having *this* conversation again."

"Once again because you don't want to discuss something it doesn't get discussed."

"I don't want to discuss it? This seems to be all we have discussed for the past two or three months. I'm fucking sick of it. You know how I feel about it. It's not going to change simply because we've had a few drinks. And asking your friends' opinions at the party, who are obviously going to take your side, isn't going to change my opinion either."

"No, we've started to discuss it and then the subject has been quickly changed and conveniently forgotten. And your opinion on the matter seems to have changed pretty easily since we've been together or did you think I wouldn't notice?"

"Why don't you just go to bed, you're drunk, you probably don't think you're drunk because you never do think you're drunk but you are drunk."

"I'm not drunk."

"Point proved. Okay. We'll see if you feel the same way tomorrow morning once the hangover kicks in."

"I'll tell you what. I'll have another drink now and make sure I am drunk and that way you can be right yet again."

"Fine. Can we at least change the subject now?"

"No, no we can't. This is it now. We are having this discussion now, drunk or not because I'm fed up of not knowing, of wondering all the time."

"Wondering about what? I've told you before I'm committed to you - that should be enough. We don't need anything else, we don't need the whole marriage ceremony circus."

"But I want it, I need it. And you've always known that, ever since we've been together you've known that and you agreed to it, or what passes for you agreeing to it in your always, nearly, not quite committing to anything kind of way and then at some point you decided to change your mind and you didn't bother to inform me. You just dropped hints and expected me work it out."

"It's…it's unnecessary. You've always known marriage is unimportant to me, it means nothing, it signifies nothing. You can have commitment without marriage and you have that already, what's so fucking important about gathering everyone in a room just to hear each other say something we already know."

"It does signify commitment, a greater commitment than just words. It means we're saying we will be together forever although.."

"Yeah well, didn't work out too good for your friends did it? At least three you asked for opinions at the party have been divorced and remarried."

"I was about to say that I know that isn't always the case."

"Really? You think?"

"You and I have different meanings for commitment."

"I'm not doubting that."

"We have been together for three years now. We never talk about the future. We don't even live together. I think you view commitment in terms of the here and now, that's as far as you get, the present. I want something that goes further than that. Are we ever going to live together? Are we ever going to have kids? What about the future?"

"I'll tell you what, why don't you just draw up a contract with a list of terms and conditions, you're the lawyer, you can even put in some cast iron clauses that are unbreakable."

"You're such an asshole."

"Well what do you think marriage is all about? That's all it is, a contract between two people but it means absolutely nothing. Just because a priest or some official has witnessed this contract doesn't make it anymore binding or valid, not in the real world."

"Not in your version of the real world."

"So you think when I say I'm committed to you that I'm being less truthful than if I say it in front of a priest? You're saying that when I say it, it doesn't count unless a priest is there to validate it. In other words, saying it now doesn't count but saying it during a marriage ceremony does? In effect, everything I have said on commitment doesn't mean shit unless someone priest or official gives their legal seal of approval."

"Look, you said to me once that marriage doesn't matter to you but if the person you were with felt strongly enough about it then you would do it because you loved that person. You said that because you loved that person you would respect that marriage was important to them, important enough that you would do it."

"I can't remember saying that, but okay, it does sound like something I would agree with."

"Well you did say it and I remember thinking at the time, well that's at least somehow reassuring. That was two years ago now, and my constantly trying to bring this subject up lately, as you say, should be a bell ringing in your head. It should be a big fucking warning sign."

"Here we go, an ultimatum."

"Call it what you want but there are certain things I have always wanted and marriage is one of them. You made that reassuring at the time statement two years ago, and now, to me, that means you don't love me enough because I feel strongly about marriage and you said if the person you loved felt strongly enough about it you would do it because you loved them, which in turn means all of your previous comments on commitment were either just so much bullshit or you do not love me, so which one is it?"

"Jesus, no wonder you win all of your cases."

"And that's not an answer."

"Yes I love you, no I don't want to get married. If something isn't broken just leave it the fuck alone."

"Well I can't accept that. That doesn't work for me."

"So what, that's it? You want to split up?"

"I think maybe there's no other option. I don't see any other option. I'm not going to change my mind about marriage and neither it seems are you."

"So three years of you saying you love me, what, that was just bullshit?"

"What? No of course not, I do love you."

"Well no, obviously you don't. You love the idea of marriage more than me. The priest, the ceremony, the whole circus, you love that more than me. You're saying, I love you but if you don't do this I will leave you."

"I didn't say that."

"You just did. You're saying, I love you but I will move onto the next person, fall in love again and get married because marriage is my ultimate goal above all else. You put marriage above love, above commitment, two things which you already have. In reality, all you want is a signed contract. Maybe we have different meanings for the definition of love."

"Stop twisting everything. You're twisting it so that I sound like the bad one, as if I'm completely shallow."

"It sounds like marriage is just something to be ticked off on your list of things to do during your lifetime and everything else comes second place. Fuck love and commitment, the two things that marriage is supposed to be about, that's just bullshit, the contract above all else."

"No! I want *love*. I want *commitment*! I want *security*! I want *safety*! I want to raise a family. I want to have and raise a family in house that we share. These things are important to me, they always have been. I'm not like you, I can't just drift through life, content with what I have now. I need to know that there are some definites, that there are things I can count on…"

"But there are no definites."

"Even if it's only the illusion that comes with a signed piece of paper, that's definite enough for me."

"So you don't want to split up?"

"No."

"But you want definitely to get married even though I don't?"

"Yes."

"Then one of us has to give in."

"Compromise."

"Compromise, give in, give way, call it what you want, it comes down to the same thing. One of us must give in."

The Elephant Frowned

"Because a person's word is not enough anymore. If there's nothing there, something has to be invented."

This entire play takes place in a bar between a film director and a journalist.

Journalist

"Thanks for taking the time to do this interview, I really appreciate it and I'm sorry this bar is a bit out of your way. I know you're busy promoting the new film."

Director

"Don't worry about it, I was visiting friends near here anyway and really, just now, I'm not all that busy. Anyway I Googled you. I like your writing. You seem to really do your research and you don't pander to the interviewee, which is why I agreed, I'm hoping this will be interesting."

Journalist

"Well I've heard post interviews that some people I've interviewed have complained I'm too confrontational though…. you don't mind if I begin recording do you? Good. Actually, to be honest, I really don't give a shit if I do come off as confrontational. I've had more than a few arguments with so called celebs and the piece will still get printed. Actually it's easier to sell if there is a bit of bitching."

Director

"Well thank Christ I'm not a celeb then although we can make up an argument if it'll make you happier."

Journalist

"Well you are in that celeb realm, almost, otherwise I wouldn't be interviewing you. People are interested in your work, in your films, in your private life."

Director

"Yeah but you're not going to see me in the celeb pages. My budget for each film is miniscule; I'm low rent, so to speak. Some people care, most don't give a shit. It's not like you've been sent to do this by some big newspaper. You're freelance right?"

Journalist

"But I will be trying to sell this to one of the nationals, weekend supplements, definitely good for your profile."

Director

"Well whatever. I just mean I'm not high profile. I make small films that some people want to see but I've also been slated a lot of the time for them."

Journalist

"And yet others say you're one to watch out for. Up and coming is the term I keep hearing."

Director

"Yeah I've done six films and I'm still up and coming at the age of 35. I doubt any other directors are shitting themselves that I'm going to steal their box office whenever I bring out a new film."

Journalist

"You know, we've met before although I doubt you'd remember it. Oh great, wine, I could do with a large glass."

Director

"Really? When was this?"

Journalist

"Clapham Common, last year. They were showing an open air screening of, I've forgotten the name of the film actually, anyway I noticed you sitting alone. I came over and asked for a hit of the joint you were smoking."

Director

"And?"

Journalist

"Yeah you give me a hit but you didn't say a word. Didn't even look up, just held the joint out to me."

Director

"Sounds like me, I was pretty drunk that night as well. Can't even remember the film either."

Journalist

"I thought you were quite standoffish at the time but now you say you were drunk as well as stoned I understand."

Director

"If I was being standoffish I wouldn't have given you the joint."

Journalist

"But you do have a reputation of being, how can I put this, aloof, arrogant, rude even."

Director

"Really? I don't know why. I'll speak to anyone. Where did you hear that?"

Journalist

"I'm just fishing actually. I was on IMDB and read some comments from a few people who claimed to have met you and said you had acted like an asshole."

Director

"A reliable source then."

Journalist

"No, like I said just fishing. Sorry, I just wanted to get a reaction. I don't use IMDB comments, don't worry."

Director

"I'm not worried for me. I'd be more worried for your career if you did use those sorts of sources in your articles."

Journalist

"You're not worried about the public's perception of you?"

Director

"Fuck no. You mean perception after reading a comment online or a newspaper article about me? If you're putting yourself in the public eye you have two choices, to read all this stuff and deal with it or simply never read it. I don't want to spend a huge amount of time trying to defend and justify myself. Life's too short. People are going to believe what they want to believe and they'll make up the rest anyway, there's nothing you can really do about that."

Journalist

"And you never read your reviews or read interviews that you've done. I find that hard to believe."

Director

"Then don't believe it and you've just proved my point."

Journalist

"But you Googled my previous articles before agreeing to this interview. You must have wanted to see what sort of writer I was. If you care about how I portray you in interviews then it follows you care about how you are seen by the public."

Director

"And from your writing I felt that you seemed pretty honest. If I'm an asshole then I'll come across as an asshole, if I'm not, judging by your previous interviews, you won't turn me into one just to sell more copy. Anyway, whether I am an asshole or not doesn't have anything to do with my work."

Journalist

"You write and direct your own work. Your films are social commentary, so going by that, you put your own views into your films. I would say that at least all of your films have what I would call vitriolic characters, many are outright assholes, people you really wouldn't want to spend any amount of time with. And I'm not saying that's a bad thing. But isn't your work heavily influenced by your own outlook on life?"

Director

"As in, do I see all other people as vitriolic assholes? No of course not. Not all of them anyway."

Journalist

"You've been accused by some of being misanthropic."

Director

"Really? I find that funny actually."

Journalist

"Well how about misogynistic."

Director

"That's also funny. There are just as many male characters who are assholes in my films as females. I don't differentiate. The characters, when I'm writing the script, could be played by either a male or a female."

Journalist

"You don't differentiate between the sexes when writing? You don't think men and women view sex, love, emotions, differently?"

Director

"But I'm not interested in that. I've mostly concentrated on the games people play with each other during relationships, manipulation to be precise. There are people who play games and people who don't. That's mostly what I've been interested in. The ones who do play these games mostly want to dominate the other, they want to win to obtain their goal, whatever their goal is at whatever cost, even if it costs the relationship. These games can be played by men or women, there's no difference."

Journalist

"How do you view these games, manipulation, in relationships?"

Director

"They're an act of war usually."

Journalist

"An act of war?"

Director

"The sweetness and light part of the relationship is over once the manipulation has begun. Once you have entered into that territory there's no going back, it's a choice. One person has decided they are going to use manipulation to get what they want and it's an act of war between two people.

Journalist

"Which is precisely how I view your films. They focus on the war of the sexes, people ripping each other to pieces by the end of the film."

Director

"Yeah, they're not Disney films I guess."

Journalist

"I felt physically and mentally drained at the end of your last film. I didn't want to have to see or think about those characters ever again."

Director

"Good."

Journalist

"That was your intention?"

Director

"Well at least you felt something right? I wanted to fuck the minds of the audience up a bit, true, but it depends on the audience. Not everyone is going to feel drained by it. Some will be bored, some will be disgusted and some will simply be entertained."

Journalist

"And many will never want to see another one of your films again. Do you think about that?"

Director

"Not really. In the same way that I don't care about bad reviews, I do not care if some people would rather go see a nice romantic comedy instead of my films. Each to their own. Fuck it if they can't take reality."

Journalist

"Entertaining is definitely not a word I would use for your films. Sitting being emotionally pummelled for two hours. And it's not a reality I relate to actually."

Director

"But it is a part of reality, maybe not yours……but…..wait ..you're telling me you've never used manipulation with people to get what you want?"

Journalist

"I probably have once or twice but it's not a way I would want to live my life, too tiring, and I really don't think I do it now, not that I'm aware of."

Director

"Not that you're aware of. Some people aren't aware they are using manipulation to get what they want. For some people it's almost instinctual. They've played these games since they were young, they've seen their parents use manipulation on each other and they've learnt from it. They've probably used this type of manipulation with their parents when they were younger as well and it worked, it has become second nature and they've kept at it their entire lives because no one has stopped them."

Journalist

"I'm aware of that. I'm just saying that it's not part of my reality. I'm not that sort of person."

Director

"Well then you're a one off aren't you?"

Journalist

"You don't believe me?"

Director

"It doesn't really matter whether I believe you does it? You're not trying to win my favour here, you're just writing a newspaper article."

Journalist

"Right. Do you ever use real life situations in your films? Situations that you yourself have experienced?"

Director

"They're mostly fiction, they're not real. There is also nothing original, these stories have been told a million times, it's just modifications."

Journalist

"So nothing from your own life whatsoever?"

Director

"I've probably taken a few lines of dialogue from real life, expanded on it. Maybe a situation I've lived through and build upon it."

Journalist

"I said before the characters seem completely unlikeable. I certainly wouldn't want to see myself portrayed on the screen in such a way."

Director

"Well none of us are the idealised versions of ourselves that we have in our own heads."

Journalist

"You portray life and people with all their warts and nastiness."

Director

"I don't try and sugar coat it, I try and keep it honest, in reality. Not every story out there has a happy ending and that's true for a lot of people. I'm not interested in writing about a guy chasing a girl in slow motion through an airport to try and win her back while a Coldplay song plays in the background."

Journalist

"So no romance in your world then?"

Director

"Maybe the next film but I doubt it."

Journalist

"What about your personal life? Any romance there?"

Director

"There is someone yes."

Journalist

"Long-term?"

Director

"Almost two years."

Journalist

"And how do they feel about your work."

Director

"I don't think they're her favourite type of films but she likes them."

Journalist

"Does she ever worry that she'll end up as a character in one of your films?"

Director

"I've never asked. I doubt it, maybe I'll ask her later."

Journalist

"If I were in a relationship with you, and having seen your films, I would be worried I'd end up as part of your work."

Director

"One of the problems of writing your own scripts is that people you know well often look to see if they can recognise themselves. I'll repeat again so you they can hear me at the back, it's fiction. Really, this interview is going to be repetitious if you don't take my word for it."

Journalist

"Maybe it's just that your films seem so realistic. Or at least other reviewers have said so."

Director

"And some have said that they were a steaming puddle of pretentious putrid piss that they would never want to step foot in intentionally again. It's all just opinion."

Journalist

"Some have also complained about the use of bad language in your films."

Director

"People use bad language."

Journalist

"Do you? In life I mean."

Director

"Not frequently but when the need arises yes."

Journalist

"The word cunt is used a lot from male to female characters in your films."

Director

"And the word prick is used a lot from female to male characters, your point being?"

Journalist

"It's quite an offensive word. Probably the most offensive word used against a woman and usually used sparingly in films. Yet you used it in The Elephant Frowned a total of 32 times."

Director

"You certainly do your research. Did you count them?"

Journalist

"It's on the internet."

Director

"There are a lot of cunts on the internet. Look, I'm not offended by bad language, a great many people are not offended by bad language. In the context of the film it was, to my mind, realistic. It was to show anger from one character to another, and at times hatred."

Journalist

"The word cunt was used to convey hatred?"

Director

"Yes."

Journalist

"Do you use that word in your own life?"

Director

"No I don't, not in that context anyway."

Journalist

"To convey hatred?"

Director

"Yes. I wouldn't use that word against someone to convey hatred. I don't think bad language is shocking. I'm not sure what you are getting at?"

Journalist

"I'm trying to get to the realism of your films, to the heart of them. You write them, yet you claim never to use that word in that context in real life. But you say your films are honest and realistic."

Director

"Yes certain people do use that word, it doesn't mean I do. Directors who make films about bank robberies don't go out and rob fucking banks. It's fiction but I know people who swear, who use the word cunt towards others in a derogatory way and in other contexts. It's not exactly a hidden club. They maybe don't use it in your world but I also know people who can use the word fuck as a noun, adjective and verb all in the same sentence."

Journalist

"So although you work is *fiction* you *do* use people and situations and dialogue from your own life when writing your script?"

Director

"If I hear a line of dialogue or can remember some situation that I can use that will enhance or add to or work well in the film then yes I will use it."

Journalist

"With no regard or thought to the people who said it in the first place? Do you think everyone is fair game to be placed in a script or story? Everything out there is up for grabs?"

Director

"In all honesty, even though the majority of my work is fiction, yes. What do you think blogging is about, or what you do is about? There's no privacy anymore. People sit and eavesdrop on other people's conversations and the next day it's on the internet for other people to read, and for what? More pageviews. So you can sell some more of your bullshit interviews to bullshit newspapers. We're all just feeding off each other and don't tell me you don't know this, you're not that naïve. "

Journalist

"But you agreed for me to interview you. The people you place in your films, the characters based on so and so, have not agreed, unless you asked them first to use that line of dialogue or situation that occurred previously."

Director

"I'd call it creative licence. I don't feel as if I need anyone's permission to use a sentence or a conversation, people don't copyright conversations."

Journalist

"What about creative responsibility?"

Director

"What about it?"

Journalist

"Being creatively responsible, knowing that what you put out there can have an influence or an effect on others. The way they think, the way they feel."

Director

"Well that's the point of creating something to make people think and feel, to give another point of view to a story. As the writer and director I ultimately have responsibility and accountability for my own work but after each film is finished and out there it's really out of my hands as to how people react to it."

Journalist

"And you have had your fair share of negative press, plenty of backlash, which can also be good to bring in an audience."

Director

"Like I said, I don't read reviews."

Journalist

"Do you ever think that maybe sometimes some of your audience are coming for the wrong reasons? They're not coming to your films to witness a searing in-depth analysis on relationships but they are simply coming to witness human behaviour at its worst. Your films are a release. After a hard week of dealing with assholes at work or at home, your films give them characters to which they can direct all of that hate and anger towards?"

Director

"Well that release is not a bad thing. I guess it's better to do that than to go out, get drunk and beat the shit out of someone. Of course there is also the view that certain members of the audience can relate to the characters."

Journalist

"And?"

Director

"Well they may see these harmful relationships on the screen, recognise it and decide to make a change. Or they may recognise a character's behaviour up on the screen, relate to it, and again, decide to make a change before it's too late."

Journalist

"Kind of like a low cost relationship guidance session?"

Director

"If you like, although it's not my intention when writing the script. I'm not interested in the aftermath of the film, only the actions the characters are taking in relation to one another."

Journalist

"People lying to each other is a big part in your films, it's almost overly moralistic sometimes how much you use this theme."

Director

"Yeah that is a theme I'm interested in I suppose in terms of the way people interact with each other. Lying, to me, is very interesting, it's a big part of life, especially with couples, and especially with certain couples who appear outwardly, and to each other, to have these perfect, honest relationships. But I don't think I'm overly moralistic, people lie every day and it doesn't mean it's a bad thing."

Journalist

"Such as sparing someone's feelings instead of telling a truth you know may hurt them?"

Director

"Of course. The thing about lying is it's like creating your own world, controlling your own little world. A tiny innocent, or as some people call them white lie, can lead eventually to the break-up of a relationship. If the other person in the relationship knows the person has lied, no matter if it was with good intentions, then it's the beginning of the breakdown of trust. A profile or a picture is being continually formed of the two people in a relationship, and the lies, big and small, add to that profile."

Journalist

"Then you're saying we are all judging each other continually."

Director

"Well the other thing about lying is that the liar is banking on two things when telling the lie. They are hoping that the person being lied to is gullible enough to believe, and it's also not even that they think they are gullible, it's that they know the person they are lying to well enough that they know the person won't push it any further because they know the person they are lying to wants to believe the lie."

Journalist

"Because the person being lied doesn't want to rock the boat?"

Director

"Exactly. They would rather live with the lie, believe it, ignore it than push for the truth and begin what could lead to the destruction of that particular relationship. Again, it's an act of war and it's up to the other person to decide whether or not it's worth retaliating after weighing up the consequences in regards to what they have to gain against what they have to lose."

Journalist

"And people believe what they want to believe."

Director

"When it comes to lies some people are like that, they will believe them if it makes life easier for them. Usually lying makes life easier for the liar, and at the moment the lie is being told, it makes life easier for the person being lied to. The seasoned liar will know all this and will tell the person being lied to exactly what they want to hear."

Journalist

"Lying is a win win situation for all involved."

Director

"Only if you are comfortable taking the easy route through life I guess. If you keep giving the appearance of believing lies then I guess you are allowing the person who is lying to you to build up one of your personal profile traits as that of gullibility."

Journalist

"And of course believing all these lies actually means, to some extent, you are living in a fictional world, a world built on lies."

Director

"Many people do it."

Journalist

"You must have some background to draw on for all this, some experience. Either lying or being lied to?"

Director

"No one goes through life without doing either at some point or other, well I don't believe so anyway."

Journalist

"So in the past have you pushed for the truth? If you were being lied to?"

Director

"I would hope so. I also don't think I tend to lie much, I don't see the point in it. To me, you are basically making life harder. I remember seeing an interview with an actress, I think it was Debra Winger, where she told the interviewer that she had told her children, if you don't lie you have less to remember."

Journalist

"So you are saying don't lie because it's wrong, but don't lie because it makes life easier?"

Director

"Well it's not my job to say what's wrong or right. If I did that I would setting myself up as extremely judgemental. People do all sorts of thing for different reasons."

Journalist

"But as the creator of these fictional films you are being, in some way, judgemental."

Director

"Well that's your opinion, it's not mine. I'm just presenting a story and the audience can decide. You seem to have decided that I'm being judgemental on the people in the film."

Journalist

"But of course you're being judgemental. You're standing up on a hill saying look at this, look at the way these people behave, isn't it atrocious? Then once you've released the film you step back, you don't read your reviews, you don't feel the need to justify or defend your actions."

Director

"Again, that's your opinion not mine."

Journalist

"People say that when they don't want to continue with a discussion, there's no retaliation just, well that's your opinion."

Director

"Well what would you like me to say? It's your opinion."

Journalist

"I think you are judging me right now. I think you have built up a profile of me based on my questions."

Director

"Then it's a good job you are not the one being interviewed isn't it? Although most interviews I read today seem to say more about the interviewer than the interviewee."

Journalist

"Well what judgement have you come up with on me?"

Director

"I would say impression not judgement."

Journalist

"And?"

Director

"Well from the discussion today I would say you don't like my films, you think they are judgemental and the characters and plotlines disgust you. I think that if you have such an intense dislike of them then you must be able to relate to them in some way but that you are just not admitting it to yourself. Somewhere, inside, they strike a nerve and you would rather they didn't."

Journalist

"So you think I am lying to myself?"

Director

"Not really lying, blanking out. Ignoring what you don't like."

Journalist

"So if people do not like your films then they are simply ignoring the fact that they can actually relate to them, deep down. You have managed, through your work to reach everyone on some level. People are simply lying if they don't like your films? That's incredibly egotistical."

Director

"No I said *you*, going by the discussion we have had today. But now you're looking for a headline that will draw in readers. That's shoddy journalism, you're trying to put words into my mouth."

Journalist

"I'm a shoddy journalist as well as lying to myself because I didn't like your film? It doesn't come much more judgemental than that."

Director

"I didn't say you were a shoddy journalist. You asked me what judgement I had made of you from the short time we have spent together and then you didn't like my conclusion."

Journalist

"Because I don't agree with your conclusion. I think you are way off base. I don't like your films because I cannot relate to them in any way, it's as simple as that, not because deep down they strike a nerve somewhere. I know some people are like that but it's not part of my world. You have simply created my character as you would for the characters in your films, and this is why, as I said before, I wouldn't like to end up as a character in one of your films because they are basically an extension of your personality and how you view and judge the world."

Director

"If you don't want to end up as a character in one of my films then be nicer."

Journalist

"As you are?"

Director

"Am I being an asshole to you here?"

Journalist

"You're trying not to be because you are portraying an image to the public."

Director

"As opposed to?"

Journalist

"As opposed to reality – not the idealised versions of ourselves that we all carry in our heads."

Director

"And the reality is?"

Journalist

"You called me a cunt once, actually not just once but many times."

Director

"I've never even met you…"

Journalist

"The night we met at the open air cinema you were *extremely* drunk and stoned. When I asked for a hit of your joint you asked me to sit down beside you and we shared more than a few joints and finished a bottle of vodka you had. We then went back to my place for more drinks. Do you remember any of that?"

Director

"Why didn't you say this when we met today?"

Journalist

"When we got back to my place you persistently tried to fuck me and when I refused you called me a cocktease, a mutherfucker and a cunt. I'm not sure if you called me a cunt 32 times but your abuse lasted for what seemed at least as long as one of your tedious films before one of my neighbours helped me to throw you out of my house."

Director

"I'm not the first person to be drunk and make an asshole out of themselves and not remembering isn't lying."

Journalist

"Aren't you ashamed of being that drunk, being so out of control?"

Director

"Here's a deal, you forget about it this time and I'll be ashamed next time."

Journalist

"You said you never used the word cunt to convey hatred, and yet you were using it pretty freely that night and unless I'm mistaken you weren't using it as a term of endearment."

Director

"I told you I don't use the word in everyday life, I cannot even remember that night but I'm now beginning to see why you were so persistent in setting up this interview."

Journalist

"Because I thought this backstory would probably make for a good interview."

Director

"A good fucking interview? You waited a year after we had first met to get in contact to interview me knowing what had happened that night. You made absolutely no mention of us meeting or what had happened during your email and phone call to me and then you spring this on me now during an interview. You who claim you're never manipulative."

Journalist

"Well if you can't appreciate it then no one can."

Journalist

"What I appreciate is that we have two different takes on that night. You said that you were smoking and drinking, so how do I know that your perception of what happened is the truth?"

Journalist

"Well actually I could have said anything I wanted, I could have made it out to be a lot worse than it actually was because you can't remember that night. But I also have my neighbour to back me up."

Director

"You cannot honestly be considering printing this?"

Journalist

"Of course, why not? It's not like you're going to sue me."

Director

"If I was really bothered I probably could."

Journalist

"But why? You don't care about public perception. You let people believe what they want to believe."

Director

"You wanted to interview me to do this hatchet job not because you hate my films but because I got drunk and called you a cunt a few times. That's the reality here. I didn't prepare for a journalist with an ulterior motive to her story. My being drunk that night has nothing to do with my work. Be a fucking professional."

Journalist

"And there are no ulterior motives behind your films? Not the slightest little bit of you taking revenge on some of the relationships you have been in? Making people see your side of the story and only your side? You're saying that what I'm telling you might not be true because it's my perception, in that case your version tops all, all of the time."

Director

"You want to tell your own version, make your own fucking film."

Journalist

"You know how I recognised you that night?"

Director

"What?"

Journalist

"At the open air cinema. Do you know how I recognised you?"

Director

"How would I know, I didn't think we'd even met before."

Journalist

"Because I was friends with Margit, remember her, you dated for six months. A girl who ended up as a character in one of your *fictional* films. The film hadn't been released when we met in the park that night. But when it was released she did recognise herself and was fucking horrified over how you portrayed her, although, according to Margit you're portrayal of her stands up to your testament that your characters are a complete work of fiction."

Director

"Jesus Christ it is fiction. If it was such an inaccurate portrayal of her, a work of fiction, then why was she horrified? How did she know it was supposed to be her? This makes no sense."

Journalist

"There were clues throughout the film. Certain habits she had, mannerisms, lines of dialogue, she said it was definitely meant to be her."

Director

"So Margit, from Switzerland, who I split up with and who now works as waitress went to see my film and saw, up on the screen, the South American language teacher who at one point kills her boyfriend's dog and then attempts suicide by driving her car into a river when drunk, none of which Margit did, Margit saw this and thought, wow that's me up there on the screen, how could this bastard do this to me?"

Journalist

"I believe her. I know her well enough and I recognised her as well in the film. I think you actually think that by changing large parts of the character you can disguise who they actually are. That by doing that it becomes fiction."

Director

"I fucking give up. Are you sure you are the same journalist who wrote those previous interviews? Believe me, you will never sell this interview anywhere if you intend to use this completely surreal story within a story."

Journalist

"Which will attest to my shoddy journalism."

Director

"If Margit saw herself within the film then I'm sorry, I don't know what to tell you, it wasn't intentional."

Journalist

"No? And yet you were nowhere to be seen in the film."

Director

"Maybe I was in the film. Are you sure I wasn't the one legged belly dancer in the nightclub scene? I probably missed that one but your powers of perception are so acute that I bow to your judgement."

Journalist

"Sorry, could I have some background info before finishing. You've been seeing your girlfriend for what, two years now, yet we met at the open air showing about a year ago was it? I just want to link this in with your theory on lying."

Director

"This interview is over."

Journalist

"Okay thanks. I just need a headline. How about, the first time we met, he called me a cunt. At least it will back up your claims of realism."

Director

"I'm past caring. I'll be surprised if that thing sees the light of day. And another thing, you know what, you are a cunt. And I'm not saying that to convey anger or hatred, it's simply a fact, it seems I was able to tell that the first night we met. This entire thing is gossip, fiction. Why interview me? You could have made the entire thing up yourself…well I hope someone buys it because……wait, hold on a minute, hold on a minute."

Journalist

"Yes, obviously I've completely misunderstood you. That must happen a lot. What are you writing?"

Director

"I've got a great idea for a script."

Film Director (walking into the set)

"Cut. Okay guys that was great."

Male Actor

"Are you going to use that one. I cannot keep doing these long fucking takes, they are killing me."

Film Director

"We need a rewrite on some of those lines."

Female Actor

"How many more times before you're happy? This is the sixth version we've done."

Film Director

"We're aiming for realism, whatever it takes. It's got to be believable."

Female Actor

"It needs something. More swearing perhaps – I'm being sarcastic in case you can't tell. And are you going to change the title? The Elephant Frowned, what does that even mean?"

Film Director

"No idea. According to the writer that's the beauty of it. The audience can read whatever they want into it."

The Seawall

"You're here. I've been waiting for you."

"Waiting for me?"

"Well I thought maybe, you know, you'd show up today. I wasn't sure so I hung around for a while."

"It is a nice day to hang around."

"Well the day's almost over."

"I know but at least I made it right? And it's a beautiful time of day, just as the evening's coming in. I like the colours."

"I know, everything's so blue, amazing. The sea looks like ice. I feel as if I could walk across it."

"Have you been waiting long?"

"Long enough."

"You should give me your phone number then I can call and you won't have to wait around in the cold."

"Let's just keep it like this for the moment, for now at least."

"Why?"

"I don't mind waiting. I like turning up wondering if you're going to be here or not. I like the anticipation."

"Okay. For now."

Garry Crystal is a writer living in Scotland. His short stories and articles have appeared in print and online including Expats Post, The Adirondack Review, Turnrow Journal, Roadside Fiction and Orato.

His first Novel, Leaving London, was released in 2014. If you have liked this short story, or even if you haven't, please take the time to leave a review on Amazon. That would be very much appreciated.

There is also a Pay What You Want option for both books on garrycrystal.blogspot.com

Thank you for reading.

Printed in Poland
by Amazon Fulfillment
Poland Sp. z o.o., Wrocław